PRAISE FOR PAMEROY MYSTERY SERIES

"The Pameroy mysteries never disappoint! I love how history gets mixed into the present. After reading this book, I really feel like I know Lillia and her Grauntie. Great read. Can't wait for the next!"

"What a fun mystery! I feel like I am right there with Lillia and Charlie during their adventures. Humorous, lighthearted and quite a page turner! I will definitely be recommending this one every chance I get!"

"Drawn into this book right from the beginning! My thirteen-year-old niece has read both books in this series and loved them. So, it's been nice that we've both enjoyed and can chat about them! Great read not just for tweens."

UNSETTLED THINGS

A PAMEROY MYSTERY

BRENDA FELBER

ISBN:978-0-9909092-0-0 paperback

ISBN:978-0-9909092-1-7 eBook

Cover Design – eBook Launch

Publisher's Cataloging-in-Publication data

Names: Felber, Brenda, author.

Title: Unsettled things : a Pameroy mystery / Brenda Felber.

Series: Pameroy Mystery

Description: Schofield, WI: Laughing Deer Press, 2015.

Identifiers: ISBN 978-0-9909092-0-0 (pbk.) | 978-0-9909092-1-7 (ebook)

Summary: The ghost of a lady in white, contacts imagineer Lillia Pameroy. She wants Lillia reunite her two children, separated decades ago by tragedy.

Subjects: LCSH Friendship--Juvenile fiction. | Family--Juvenile fiction. | Psychics--Juvenile fiction. | Land Between the Lakes (Ky. and Tenn.)--History--Juvenile fiction. | Barkley, Lake (Ky. and Tenn.)--History--Juvenile fiction. | Kentucky Lake (Ky. and Tenn.)--History--Juvenile fiction. | Cemeteries--Juvenile fiction. | Ghosts--Juvenile fiction. | Ghost stories. | Mystery fiction. | BISAC JUVENILE FICTION / Mysteries & Detective Stories | JUVENILE FICTION / Horror & Ghost Stories | JUVENILE FICTION / Paranormal, Occult & Supernatural

Classification: LCC PZ7.F33375 Un 2015 | DDC [Fic]--dc23

To my children and grandchildren,
My joy and my inspiration.

CONTENTS

QUOTE TO PONDER

"And above all, watch with glittering eyes the whole world around you because the greatest secrets are always hidden in the most unlikely places. Those who don't believe in magic will never find it."

Roald Dahl

1

LILLIA

I swatted at the annoying wasp buzzing around my ankles. Birds bickered in tree branches overhead. A harsh screechy whine came from an old rusty bicycle as it sped past on the street. The rider bending over the wide-spread handlebars caught my eye as she passed. I tried to stare her down, but she tipped her head back and laughed.

You are not real. All of you leave me alone. Right now!

A pretty, young mother pushing her baby stroller by on the sidewalk nodded at me with a warm smile. Down the street, a dog barked twice. The birds started chirping sweetly.

Hey it worked! I told the imagining to clear out and it did. Normal twelve-year-olds don't have to worry about imaginings. On this trip, that is what I wanted to be...a normal kid.

"Lillia," Grauntie Nora called from the porch, "Lillia

sweetie, are you finished with that ice cream? I want you to come on up here and join us. A couple of ladies for you to meet."

"Be right there." I stalled, trying to avoid meeting any more of Grauntie's people today. But she didn't have to know that. If I told her I was in a leave me alone kind of mood, she would start in trying to change it, to cheer me up.

Sooo...I pushed myself up off the grass, deciding I might as well get this over. I stepped up to the sidewalk leading to the big house. The paver stones no longer lay tight in the ground. Looked like they had been settling into their own uneven, tippy shape for years and no one bothered to fix them.

Big grumpy trees guarded the old weathered house. Their reaching limbs covered the whole yard, ready to grab anyone they chose.

Grauntie Nora was giving me her hurry along now wave.

The overflowing flower baskets and the wicker rockers made the porch seem so inviting. I climbed the porch steps to join the group.

"Lillia, please meet Ms. Elvira Clepchek and Miss Margaret Lewis. Ladies, this is my grandniece Lillia. Her dear departed grandfather was my brother," Grauntie said, presenting me with a flourish of her arm.

Ms. Elvira, a big round piece of woman, said, "Welcome to White Cliff Landing. Suppose our little town is too quiet for a city gal?"

Was I supposed to answer that somehow? First off, I do not come from such a big city. Second, I loved small towns. Guess I paused too long because Grauntie answered it for me.

"Oh, not at all. Lillia loves country living. She loves camping and fishing. Why last year we stayed for a whole week in a tent in the forest."

"Well then young gal, hope your visit goes well."

"Thank you, ma'am," I said.

I turned to the other woman. She reached out her small wrinkled hand. I'm not big on shaking hands, no kid really is. I extended my hand because it was awkward not to. She took hold of it and hung on.

It started up again. I could see the flowers, porch posts, and sidewalk tunneling away. The sounds of birds, traffic passing by, and normal neighborhood stuff started to muffle and slow down, getting shuffled and mixed up. Shook my head and blinked my eyes.

The old lady was saying, "Nice to meet you Lillia. I too hope you enjoy your visit here in our little town." Her voice went up at the end and a wrinkle formed on her forehead as if she could tell something weird had just happened to me. "I look forward to seeing you and your grandaunt this evening." She winked and gave my hand a squeeze before she released it.

"Sorry, I can't make it. With this extra weight I carry

my knees have been giving me such grief," Elvira said, breaking into any response I might have chosen to give.

"Lillia, cat got your tongue?" Grauntie asked. I started to answer but she kept right on chatting. "We will surely miss you, Elvira. Miss Margaret, would you like someone to come here to walk into town with you?"

"No, I'll be fine until Main Street, but the steep walk down to the marina might be best with a hand to grab should my feet decide to fail me. I would hate ending up sliding down to your houseboat on my bum!"

"We'd pull you out of the water sweetie. But, to save all of that, how's about I ask Julia to meet up with you on Main Street?"

Glad she didn't volunteer me for that job.

"Sounds like a smart idea."

"Well, Lillia and I better be moseying on. We're stopping at Julia's for lunch, then Hattie's for flowers." Grauntie nudged me, "Say your goodbyes Lillia."

"My goodbyes." My only words spoken so far.

Grauntie laughed. "She's always picking on me like that. But I love it. We have fun together, don't we?"

Miss Margaret added "Lillia, do you know how lucky you are to have such a sweet grandaunt? She's a gem."

I answered, "Yep, she's a gem." She really is, but we have different ideas of what our time together should be about. She doesn't chill enough for me. Always telling me about the place we're staying. Then, the social whirl of random friends she makes. Like this dinner tonight with a bunch of people I don't know. Oh well.

With a goodbye wave, we left the Tulliver Home for the Aged and set off down the hill toward Main Street.

"Lillia sweetie, look out over the rooftops. See the lake and then the land on the other side?"

Even though I couldn't see what Grauntie Nora was talking about, I nodded and she kept on talking.

LATE NIGHT ARRIVAL

"That strip of land is called Land Between the Lakes. Years ago, two rivers were dammed up to control devastating flooding. Those dams created two lakes. Then the government turned the land between them into a recreational area. Isn't it beautiful?"

Lillia nodded. "Sure Grauntie. It's beautiful."

Grauntie Nora thought Lillia could use some distractions. She's not herself. "Hey, I know, let's take the houseboat to another marina for an overnight stay."

"The houseboat can move? I thought it stayed right in the marina where it's parked. I mean it has plants on it and dishes in the cupboards. Don't they tip over or break?" Lillia asked.

"Well, first the boat is docked, not parked. It's very steady in the water and moves across the lake just fine.

Course I wouldn't take it out in bad weather. We won't even break a glass on our journey to LBL."

"LBL?"

"Land Between the Lakes. Like I was explaining, it's..."

"Oh yeah. Got it. Sorry, forgot for a sec," Lillia said.

"Now wasn't that a gorgeous house where Miss Margaret lives? Could use a bit of touching up, though. It was once the home of Gustave Tulliver, the owner of a local iron ore plant. The family lost their money in the early 1900's and left the area. They abandoned their beautiful house."

"Where do you learn all this stuff Grauntie? And why?"

"Ah sweetie, I'm a curious person. The house had been sitting empty for years. Knowing Elvira, I can tell you you'll be hearing the story of how her mother saved the house from burning down."

"Okay, thanks for the heads up."

"Afterward, the village decided to clean it up and make it a home for elderly people who don't have anywhere else to go."

"Like Miss Margaret?"

"That's right. She's lost touch with all of her family. So now she, Elvira, the Smithton brothers and two other elderly ladies live there."

Lillia is tuning out Nora thought...information overload. She will be here for a few more days so just let her relax and try to forget about the troubles back home. Time to learn about this area another day. After all, she only got in last night.

* * *

It had been late when Nora saw her nephew's car enter the marina. She reached out to give him a hello hug but he said, "Hey Aunt Nora, hang on, let me get Lillia out of the car before she wakes up."

Always hurrying, she thought. Adam needs to slow down. Following him into the houseboat, she watched as Adam put the still sleeping Lillia in the top bunk and kissed her cheek before saying, "They sure do appear innocent when they're sleeping."

Walking out of the room, he had rubbed the back of his neck and rolled his shoulders. "Too bad they lose it when they wake up. Heck of a long drive. Charlie's asleep too, thank God. Want to finish the drive to Mike's in peace."

His eyes scanned the main living area of the boat. "So this is your latest abode? Small huh? Guess you would call it cozy, though, right Auntie Positive?"

"It is cozy to me Adam." His comments could be so cutting sometimes. And what is wrong with cozy? "So how is Jennifer doing with the pregnancy?"

"Not so good. Morning sickness again, worse than last time. Haven't told the kids they're getting a new baby sister yet. So hope you can manage to keep that to yourself while Lillia's with you."

"Of course. But why not tell them?"

"Because that darn fear of Jen's is raising its ugly head again. I hope that she can pull herself together soon. Should be a happy time, but she's not there yet I guess. To be honest, I'm tired too. Tired of dealing with all the tension and arguing. This trip will be a much-needed break in the action."

"I'm so sorry to hear that. I imagine Lillia's confused about what's happening too. Don't you think?"

"Oh, I know she is. Jen said she was a little brat about getting ready to come here today."

"Should I try to get Lillia to talk about what happened?"

Nora hated trying to dance around figuring out what Adam and Jennifer wanted and did not want her to do. Nora knew she didn't want to be the relative from hell by forcing her ideas on them, but gosh almighty, hard to agree with how they handled things sometimes.

"Let's play it by ear. Gonna try to clear my head with a few beers and a little fishing. Escape. All this crap will be waiting for me when I get back."

"Adam, please."

"Don't give me a hard time. Remember I'm not your little nephew anymore. Besides, you don't know how bad it's been."

"You don't have to use that tone nor that language."

"Sorry Auntie. Love you."

Nora and Adam shared a quick awkward hug.

"Love you too. I'll be sure Lillia calls home in a day or two."

Adam ducked back under the doorframe and stepped onto the houseboat deck. He yanked his cell phone out and checked the screen, his fingers sliding over the face, before jamming it back in his pocket. He returned to the car with his sleeping son inside and drove away.

* * *

That had been only a few hours ago. Lillia is obviously troubled about something. Have patience, not too many questions. Let her settle in a bit. Don't be such a worrywart. Enjoy this beautiful sunny day with your wonderful grandniece next to you.

3

LILLIA

I knew she meant well, but seriously, do I need to know everything about every place? I had other things on my mind right now.

We continued our walk downhill toward the village.

"Grauntie, how come Dad didn't wake me to say bye last night? Bet he couldn't wait to dump me so he could go fishing with Charlie."

"Don't be silly. He wanted you to stay asleep because it was so late."

I tripped and Grauntie reached out to put her arm around me. "Did you get enough sleep last night sweetie?"

"I guess. I liked being up high in a bunk with the little round window right there."

I do not like lying to Grauntie Nora. But what is the sense of having her worry too? Why did she need to know I had tossed and turned all night?

* * *

Mom and Dad have had some doozy fights the past few days. Don't tell me, hey watch your tone...listen to yourselves. Slammed doors. Angry silences.

Mom has been acting so weird toward me again. I try to stay low, out of her radar, until her mood has passed.

Yesterday, though, I was ticked off. Enough is enough.

She thinks I don't remember asking about the baby doll, but I do.

I was only a little kid then. None of it was my fault. I did not do anything to hurt my sister.

It has to be all of that again.

This was not fair. Charlie and Dad were going fishing without me. No Lillia. Bad little Lillia. She is sent away. Mother Dear wants to be alone.

She knew I was mad, but she was getting her way, so she started trying to be nice to me.

She tried to help pick out clothes to pack. I grabbed T-shirts and shorts and threw them in the duffle bag.

She asked, in her sweetest mommy voice, what snacks I wanted for the trip.

"Whatever," I answered, slamming the porch door on my way out.

When lunchtime came, I didn't eat.

When Dad got home, things kicked into high gear.

Dad finished packing the car. Mom brushed a kiss against his cheek. She gave Charlie a big bear hug, picking him up off his feet. When she got to me, she hugged me too, holding me for a few seconds.

I stood there taking her fake hug.

Behind her, I saw the lights on in the kitchen and Tucker up against the window, his paws on the sill.

My head lay in the cradle of her neck and I found myself snuggling in. Her scent filled my nose while her hair tickled it.

I started to say I was sorry...that I had been mean to her, but she pushed me away, saying, "Be good and say hi to Grauntie for me."

So much for that.

Dad, Charlie, and I left. Crouched in the back seat of the car, hugging my knees tight against my chest, I stared out the window, watching as the flat Kansas plains rolled past. Driving for hours, the view out my window cast in darkness as we entered the Ozark Mountains. Dad stopped for hamburgers and fries. I didn't want to talk or think anymore, so I tried to fall asleep as we drove into the night shadows of Kentucky.

Next thing I remembered was hearing Dad say that I was not so innocent.

* * *

My thinker sure hurt and it still does.

4

MEETING ZOE

Lillia and Grauntie Nora turned right on Main Street, heading back the way they had walked earlier this morning.

They passed the clock shop, unaware of the clockmaker in his upstairs apartment, reaching for his mug and finishing the last of the morning coffee. His stooped figure turned to the small kitchen sink where he scraped toast crumbs off an old chipped plate and held it under the running water. Soon he would be making his way down the stairs to open up the TLC shop for the day.

Next door at the Pottle Ice Cream Parlor, Peter had been sitting on his outdoor bench enjoying the beautiful morning in White Cliff Landing. He never tired of the view down the hill toward the marina and out across Kentucky Lake to the LBL.

When he rose to erase yesterday's flavor of the day on

his outside signboard, he saw Nora and Lillia walking up. "Hello, again ladies. Did you have a good visit up at Tully's?"

"Yes, we did Peter. Glad you let us get such an early morning ice cream cone. I know it's silly, but we've made it a tradition for our first morning breakfast together."

"No problem. I like to get an early start. Don't sleep well anyway, so might as well be up and about doing something I say." He turned and wrote Mighty Mint Mix-up on the board as he said, "So I come down here early to get a jump on the day."

"Well then, I'm glad we took a chance and knocked on your shop window," Nora said, as she nudged Lillia in the shoulder. "Right sweetie?"

Lillia smiled. "Yes, thank you, Mr. Pottle."

Earlier, before breakfast, in the apartment above the Main Street diner, Zoe Kingman had stretched, yawned, and rubbed the sleep from her eyes.

She loved the view. Beautiful lake. No ugly row of apartments. No neighbors arguing. Nobody to hang out with, though. Bummer. Used to be able to walk out the door and bing, friends to hang with. No one had shown up here all summer. Maybe today. Who knows? Be nice when school starts. Probably a long bus ride, but at least during the school year there were kids to talk with.

Stop it Zoe Kingman! How can you possibly be wishing for school to start? Snap out of it girl.

She glanced at the clock on the way to the bathroom.

Oh darn, better get going. Late already. Mom will be waiting for me again. When Dad was with them, Mom didn't have to work. Now she worked all the time and expected help from *moi*.

The stairs creaked and squeaked as Zoe bounded down them a few minutes later.

"Hey, Mom. Sorry, I'm late. Whatcha want me to do first?"

"There you are. Sleep well?" Julia asked.

"Not bad." Zoe grabbed the cloth from her mom and took over wiping the tables by the window. "What's the special today? I'm starving."

She finished with a flourish and turned to see Mom watching her, hands on hips, smiling. She did seem a lot happier these days.

"What?" Zoe asked with a grin.

"Nothing," Julia said. "I love watching you work. When I was little and your grandparents had this diner, the Tuesday special was always macaroni and cheese. How's that sound?"

"Excellent!"

The front door of the diner opened and Zoe turned to see a woman and a girl come in. Hmmm, she looks about my age. Someone to hang out with? Sweet.

"Hi, Nora. How are you doing today?" Julia said. "And this must be your grandniece."

"I'm doing good Julia. Yes, this is Lillia. Lillia, this is Julia Kingman and her daughter Zoe."

Julia said, "Nice to meet you. Are you two going to have an early lunch?"

"May I suggest our super-duper special macaroni and cheese?" Zoe said quickly. "It's amazing!"

"Good with me Zoe. How about you Lillia?"

Lillia looked like she wasn't sure what to say, so Zoe figured she'd help her decide. "It's really really good. It was my Granny's recipe. Mom makes it with an extra crispy baked topping. Bet you'll like it. Fresh green beans with it. Don't have to eat those if you don't want of course. But I like 'em."

"Sounds good," Lillia said.

Nora said, "And Julia, I will take you up on that offer to bring something to dinner tonight."

"Oh good. What would you like?"

Zoe raised her hands in a prayer motion. "Please let it be a dessert. You make the best desserts. Please, please, please."

"Oh, you sweet talking daughter of mine. Blueberry pie okay with you Nora?"

Zoe practically shouted, "Yes, pie! And can we have ice cream with it?"

"Hey let's give a hostess a chance to approve first."

"Sounds like the perfect idea to me."

"Well, I'll bake one if my darling daughter will agree to run down to Hattie's and get some of her fresh blueberries for me."

"No problemo Mom. For your pie, I'd even pick the blueberries right off the bushes."

"I love your enthusiasm. How about you walk down to Hattie's with us after we've finished eating? I want to grab veggies for dinner and a bouquet of flowers," Nora said.

"Okay, Mom?"

"Sure," Julia said. "But first, Zoe, let's get them seated so they can eat."

An hour later, the harbormaster watched the old woman from the houseboat, the girl who arrived last night, and the Kingman girl, walk toward Hattie's farm stand.

He kept an eye on goings around here. He knew this village and the land across the lake well. Many unsettled souls had passed this way. His ancestors, the Native American Indians, walked the Trail of Tears through here. Civil War soldiers fought on this soil.

Not so very long ago there had been another unsettling time. A time that saw entire families and villages forced to move off the land.

The girl who came last night concerned him. She too seemed unsettled.

5

LILLIA

I thought the mac and cheese wasn't too bad, but nowhere near as good as what Mom makes right out of the box. Charlie and I always argue over who gets seconds. Oh and those sweet pickles she puts out too. Yum!

Forget about it Lillia, you're here now. Mom wanted to be alone...and she got what she wanted.

Seemed like Zoe wants to hang out with me. Might be fun. I hope Grauntie doesn't mind. I know she loves when we visit her, wherever she is staying. Always wants to show us lots of stuff about places. Expose us to the world as she says. She tries to cram tons of stuff into each day. Dad says do not exhaust her, she is getting old. I say, I can't keep up with her.

When the three of us got to the farm stand, Grauntie called out. "Hey friend, place keeping you busy?" A straw hat popped up from behind a pile of crates stuffed with cabbage. The person wearing it had the kind of brown wrinkled face that belongs to farmers who have spent hours working under the hot sun. Her long shirt and baggy jeans smudged with dirt. When I saw her wipe her hands on them, I wondered how she figured that was going to get her hands any cleaner.

With a huge grin, she walked out to the front counter, which was a board on some barrels. Tucking stray hair back under her hat, she gave Grauntie Nora a big hug. "Hello, there you! And what a pleasant surprise to see you too Zoe."

"Hi, Hattie. Got some big juicy blueberries?"

"Sure do. Your mom baking some pies I bet."

Zoe gave thumbs up. "For the dinner tonight."

"And I have to assume this is Lillia? You are the spitting image of your daddy when he used to come here for summer visits."

Grauntie said, "Lillia, this is my good friend Hattie. it's her boat, Lady of the Lake, we're staying on."

"Your grandaunt has been counting the days until you got here. Hope you enjoy houseboat living."

I was still trying to picture Dad when he was little. If he's is in a goofing around mood he can be tons of fun, like a little kid.

"It's nice to meet you. The houseboat is terrific. " It should be cool actually. I've stayed in so many different places with Grauntie. Usually, Charlie is with us, though. Why is this time different? Something has changed in my family. It scares me...makes me mad too. I am old enough. They can talk to me. All this hush-hush stuff. I hate it.

Green fresh smells filled my nose, like back home after Dad had cut the grass. Earthy smells like the fall leafs he raked into piles for us to jump into.

This shed looked like it has been here for lots of years. At my feet were baskets filled with jumbles of green beans. Behind Hattie, I could see boxes holding corncobs still in their husks.

"Lillia, can you pick out a bouquet of flowers for our dinner table. They're in the back, in those white pails."

Zoe piped in, "Want me to help you?"

With a nudge on my back, Grauntie said, "Sounds like a good idea. Why don't you girls pick out a bouquet together?"

Zoe said, "Look at these, they're black-eyed Susan's. Wonder who Susan was? Can people have black eyes? What do you have there Lil?"

I was holding a flower stem with delicate bluish purple flowers riding up a gently curving stalk. The flower shapes reminded me of the lilies of the valley growing around the trees back home. I took a deep swallow to still the wave of homesickness rolling through me.

"Ah, not sure Zoe. But their shape reminds me of small flowers my Mom has." Home...mom in her apron holding the door open to let Tucker come back in. Do not go there. She was glad to see you leave.

Zoe took the flower from me and waved in the air. "What kind of flowers are these?" she called out to Hattie.

Removing her straw sunbonnet, Hattie made her way to us. "Those are foxglove. Many years ago in old England, the people thought the bell-shaped flowers provided protection for small folks."

"Small folks? Like little people?" Zoe asked. "There are reality shows about little people."

"No, folks meant fairies. They called the protecting shape a glove. Folks sounds like fox, so over time, folks glove evolved into foxglove. Also, there are people who say the name has to do with witches because the flower can be deadly."

Zoe threw the stem at me. "Deadly? Witches? Nasty!"

I quickly stuck it back in the pail. I couldn't believe they didn't have a do not touch sign on it. Wish I had that hand sanitizer Mom carries in her purse.

With a laugh, Hattie said, "Let me explain. Foxglove contains digitalis. It is extracted from the dried leaves and used for heart problems. In large quantities, it can be poisonous, though."

Zoe asked "So too much a good witchy thing can be bad. And a little witchy portion might be good. Wonder what the just right portion of this foxy flower makes the best potion."

"Phew, that's a mouthful! All I know is I like the fairy story better," I said.

"Me too," Zoe echoed.

"Hey my little one, I bet you'll like the witch story better if I get heart problems!"

Crossing my arms and raising my eyebrows I said, "Hmm...?"

Grauntie shrieked. "You even have to think? Oh my gosh..."

"Oh you know you'll live to be a hundred. At the first sign of any heart problems, though, I'll march right off to the garden for the foxglove."

"Good to hear. Now how about you two put a bouquet together?"

As I bent to pick out flowers, I noticed a man watching us from the dock area. His long black hair held in a braid. He dipped his head in greeting. A quick smile popped out of me before I turned away. Never make eye contact with strangers Mom always said.

6

EVENING

In the village of White Cliff Landing, evening shift workers headed to the dam. Children ran and played outdoors in the summer night air. Pleasure boats headed back to the marina, their wakes glistening with the setting sun's light. Soft yellows and oranges, with hints of purple, filled the sky and faded into the horizon. Quiet descended across the land and the lake.

On Land Between the Lakes, the day's activities were winding down as well. The edges of the forests and fields softened and faded with the evening shadows lengthening. The woodland cricket's serenade intensified with the dusk. The campers settled in for the evening, lighting campfires to chase away the shadows.

In the gift shop at the Home Place, a living historical farm on LBL, Delcie and Virginia had cleaned out the coffee maker, swept up the wooden floors, and straightened gift items on the shelves.

Securing the front door behind them, they headed to the far edge of the parking lot where their two cars were the only ones left.

"Phewie! Wished I'd opened these car windows today," Virginia said. "Hot as an oven inside. Will feel good to put my feet up and watch my Andy Griffin reruns tonight."

"I'm planning on doing a bit of work on one of my antique dolls while I watch Medium," Delcie said as she unlocked her car.

"What's it about?"

"It's about this woman who can communicate with dead people. She works with the police to solve crimes. Of course, they give her a hard time, what with claiming she can talk to people who've passed over."

"Lordy, that sounds strange. Do you believe in all such nonsense?" Virginia asked.

"Sure, why not? Who are we to know what some folk can do? Anyway, this show was based on a real gal. Now it looks like her daughters have inherited her abilities."

"Well don't go giving yourself any bad dreams watching all that stuff," Virginia said, as she waved out her car window.

"No problem. I sleep like a baby."

Back at White Cliff Landing Zoe smelled the fresh blueberry pie fresh out of the oven. Mom had made it with her extra special crisscross crust.

"Zoe honey, can you run over to Pottle's and get ice cream now? Here's the money."

"Sure Mom. Meet you in a few minutes."

"Oh and Miss Margaret should be passing through soon too. We promised we'd wait for her and walk over to the marina together."

Already half way out the door, Zoe shouted back, "I'll watch for her.

Miss Margaret, with carefully curled hair, left Tully's. She had picked out a summery floral print dress with a pale pink sweater for tonight. "What a lovely evening," she said aloud, to no one in particular, as she strolled toward Main Street.

At Pottle's Ice Cream Parlor, Peter was on his bench, reading the local newspaper when she approached. "Why don't you look lovely tonight Miss Margaret."

With a small curtsy, she said, "Why thank you. I'm on my way to a dinner party on Lady of the Lake."

"Enjoy yourself."

"I plan to. Twilight, wine, good company. But first Peter, I'd like to buy a bit of Hagen's Point fudge to take along."

"Sure Margaret, come on in."

Zoe saw her. "Hey, Miss Margaret. Need a hand going down to the boat?"

"Sure Zoe. Grabbing some fudge. Can you wait for me?"

"No problemo! Getting ice cream, myself."

Peter cut and wrapped the fudge and handed it to Margaret. "My treat."

"How kind. Thank you. I'll be sure to let the guests know."

"Now Zoe, what can I get for you?"

Zoe said, "Vanilla ice cream, enough for pie for...how many people? Me and Miss Margaret, Mom, Nora, Lil and Hattie. Six, enough for six huge scoops."

She is such a sweet lady, all dolled up, Zoe thought. Glad she could make it. Mom had told her Margaret was all alone with no family. Kind of like us. Would be nice if she had a family. Wonder how that happens. How do you not have a family?

Julia waited outside, holding her pie box. "Ready Zoe? Oh, Margaret, you are so pretty. What a beautiful sweater."

Next door, at TLC, the clock man sat on his cracked concrete stoop outside the shop's front door. He watched the group as they left Pottle's and headed down toward the marina.

On the upper deck, Grauntie Nora and Lillia saw them approaching. The dining table was set and in the middle stood the bouquet of foxglove, daisies, and greens. Next to it, a hurricane glass held a lighted candle. Its inviting flame reached up straight and strong, lighting the flowers with a soft glow.

Sitting on the edge of the dock, leaning against the piling, the harbormaster relaxed in the cool evening breeze.

He found pleasure in the simple act of watching Mother Earth calm and settle her world.

Across Kentucky Lake, the LBL was dark against the setting sun.

7

LILLIA

I watched the candle flame, burning steadily in its glass tower. An evening breeze made the loose tendrils of Grauntie's hair dance. She leaned over to hear something Hattie was saying, nodding and smiling in agreement.

We had finished dinner and were starting dessert. The ice cream melted into puddles against the dark blue of the warm berries. Music played on the radio. Faint conversations carried over from people on other houseboats enjoying the same summer evening.

My ears picked up new sounds. Quick sharp short notes. Twangs and pops. Fiddled see-saw sounds. They vibrated through me. Guitar chords rolled and tumbled.

I found myself tapping my fingers in time to the distant music. My feet danced beneath the table. My head nodded and bopped.

Miss Margaret seemed confused. She stretched her head

up to see across the lake toward the dark shoreline. No one else seemed to notice. Zoe was licking the remaining berries off her plate. Julia was accepting compliments on her baking.

I watched as Miss Margaret pushed back her chair and stood up. She moved to a clear area on the upper deck and started a small swaying bouncy movement. Her feet took a few quick steps. Then she reached down, drew the skirt of her dress up slightly, and added short foot flicks in perfect time to the music.

Whoa...wait a minute...I was there...now I'm here. I couldn't believe it but I had risen to join her. Wait, I don't dance. She did a pattern and stopped. I repeated. Another pattern and again I followed her lead. My dance movements loosened. Waves traveled up from my feet and through my entire body.

Conversations trailed off as everyone stopped to watch us, staring with awkward, uncomfortable smiles.

A new tune, with a harmonica playing, started up. The musical notes came strong and powerful, pulled me in, then released me. Bowing and crossing in front of each other, we danced a new step. I couldn't stop smiling and neither could she. This music was fun!

It ended.

We both looked over toward a campfire on the far shore. People moved about, their shadows thrown up against a tall rock.

Were the musicians going to play another song? A sigh

of relief escaped from Miss Margaret as a song with a slower tempo began.

"Blue Moon of Kentucky Waltz," Miss Margaret said her words barely a whisper past my ears. "My daddy and his friends used to play it when I was a wee little one."

She reached to join hands with me as we began a slow rhythmic sway. With long sliding steps, we twirled in loose soft movements, going round and round.

I do not want our dizzying dance to stop. Miss Margaret was glowing.

Downbeat. Flourish. The end.

"What a beautiful song," I murmured.

She released my hands. "Oh no, they're packing up to go."

The shadowy figures stepped away from the fire and turned their backs to us. They walked behind the rock and into the dark forest.

A veil of sweet sadness rolled down over Miss Margaret's eyes as she watched them leave.

"Woo-hoo! You two were working it. Your feet were flying, all that bowing and twirling. Can you teach me?" Zoe said. "Where'd you learn to dance like that?"

Shrugging my shoulders, I glanced at Miss Margaret. She took a deep breath and winked at me before saying to everyone, "My goodness but that was fun! Hope you enjoyed our little display of toe-tapping, heel stomping, fiddle dancing done Kentucky style."

We dipped down low as we took our bows to everyone's applause.

In a soft secret voice, she said, "Thank you for sharing with me. I haven't been with my family for a very long time."

With her family? What family? She had no family.

"You are welcome."

Why was I whispering too?

8

SETTLING DOWN

The moon rose over Kentucky Lake. Low blanketing sounds of chirping crickets filled the night air. Dogs and children called in for the evening. The shifting blue glow from television screens shown from living room windows.

On Main Street, the warm white globes topping the lampposts lit the sidewalk. Inside the Main Street Diner, a small blinking red light showed the coffee maker was ready for early morning brewing.

Store windows in Pottle's and TLC were dark. From the apartment above TLC, haunting strains of violin music drifted out the open window.

The harbormaster sat on the old pier bench smoking his evening cigar. He listened as goodnights were called out to the people leaving the boat.

Crossing the dock area and heading up the hill toward

Main Street, Miss Margaret turned to wave one more goodbye to Nora, Hattie, and Julia. They all waved back, as Nora called out, "Don't be too long Lillia."

"Okay, Grauntie."

"Meet you back home honey," Julia shouted.

The words, "You got it Mom," carried faintly back up to the houseboat deck.

They sat back down to finish their wine at the open-air dinner table.

"Sometimes I think Zoe pretends she doesn't hear me. Her mind is always racing," Julia said.

"I never had children but I've heard tweens can be...hmm, how to put it? Interesting? Zoe was so thoughtful to suggest the fishing trip tomorrow. I'm glad Lillia found someone here her own age to hang around with," Nora said.

"I feel so badly for her sometimes. Zoe has always wanted a sister and I know she misses her friends back home. The divorce was so hard on us all."

"You are making a wonderful life for her here. Home is where you hang your hat and her hat rack is right inside your front door," Hattie said.

"I know, but it doesn't mean we both don't miss part of what we left behind."

"You did the best you knew." Hattie took a sip of her wine. "Miss Margaret had such a fun time. It was so lovely of you to put this together for us Nora."

Picking up the bottle, Nora reached across to pour some wine in Julia's glass. "Did you think Lillia and Margaret dancing like that was kind of odd? As though they were dancing to a different music than we heard?"

"I agree, I didn't get it either," Julia said.

"Well, whatever was happening it made me smile. Wonderful to see Lillia so full of joy. My nephew's family is a little stressed right now and I know it's affecting her."

"Do you want to talk about what's going on with your family?" Hattie asked.

"It's sort of hard to explain. It's happy news actually. Now you cannot tell Lillia yet though because Adam and Jen want to surprise her and Charlie. But...drumroll...Jen is pregnant."

"Oh Nora, what happy news. Everything all right with the pregnancy?"

"Yes. Jen is fine. Little morning sickness, but not bad."

"So what is the tension about? What is upsetting Lillia?"

Nora debated about how much to share with her friends. It was so hard to explain what had occurred eight years ago. "Something happened with Charlie's birth. He was a twin. His little sister died before she was born."

Julia gasped. "Oh my, that's awful. I'm so sorry."

"Thank you. It was an emotional time. I think that is part of what is making Jennifer so edgy now. It's like she's reliving it."

Julia added, "The sad loss of one child, along with the joy of another one's birth. Not an easy time by any measure."

"You're so right," Nora said, deciding that was enough of the story to tell right now.

She had come to accept Lillia's specialness, but not understand it. Lillia simply could not have known Charlie's twin was no longer alive when she told Jen about the doll. No one knew it then.

9

LILLIA

I held my elbow out toward Miss Margaret. She nodded and hooked on with her elbow.

I sang out, "One two three...we're off to see the Wizard, the wonderful Wizard of Oz." With that, we started a high-stepping skip toward town.

Zoe took her other arm. "We hear he's a whiz of a Wiz if ever a Wiz there was."

"The Wizard is one because, because, because, because," Miss Margaret sang.

"Because of the wonderful things he does!"

Slowing to a walk, Miss Margaret laughed. "Ah, I feel so much younger. It was wonderful to hear bluegrass music again, it sang to my heart. Took me back to being a little girl living in the Kentucky woods. You picked up the dance steps quickly I've got to say."

"I did, didn't I? It was fun. Like my feet had a mind of

their own. Wonder where it was coming from?"

Zoe looked back toward the marina lights. "Hmm, I couldn't hear the music you were dancing to."

"Well, you were too busy licking off your plate."

"Hey!" I saw her come around, ready to take a swipe at me. I ran, ducking behind a lamppost and grabbing Miss Margaret, putting her between us.

"Girls, easy! Do not put me in the middle of this. I will say, even though my hearing isn't what it used to be, I could hear the music just fine."

"You really didn't hear it, Zoe? It was sort of like St. Patrick's Day music," I said.

Zoe's eyes narrowed and with a flip of her hair, she said, "Well, sorry. Maybe I couldn't hear it because...?" She seemed to be searching for something. "Duh, I know, I was sitting right next to the radio speaker. That's why. I had other music playing. Loud. Right in my ear."

Miss Margaret quickly said, "Oh I bet that's why you didn't hear our band dear."

Zoe brightened. "But I do know about bluegrass music." She turned herself around so she was walking backward and facing Miss Margaret. "Studied it in music class last year. Let me think. A mix of blues and jazz. Brought by Scottish, Irish, English immigrants. Acoustic stringed instruments. Pretty good huh? Got an A in music class."

"Wow Zoe, careful there, here walk beside me again. You are full of information. That is right about bluegrass, it is like some of the Irish music. They were one of the groups that brought it to America. Sure was fun to hear it again."

"Ooh...maybe you were time warped, or transported by the great and powerful Oz? What about that idea?"

"Let's go with it. I time traveled to the Land of Oz for about, oh, let us say nine minutes and nineteen seconds. I like that."

"What would you ask that great and powerful Oz for if you ever get to meet him? Courage, heart, brains?" Zoe asked

"Hmmm, well he's apparently given me better hearing tonight. Perhaps less gray hair, a better memory, or losing a few extra pounds? Little things," Miss Margaret said with a lighthearted giggle.

"I hope the Wizard grants all your requests," Zoe said.

"Are you getting tired? We could walk slower," I asked as I saw Miss Margaret slow down.

She shook her head no and shrugged. "No, nothing like that. Just realized my one wish for Oz would be to find out if I still had family in these parts. Think he could do that?"

Such sadness in her voice. I remembered when she had told me how lucky I was to have my family. Was I bad to be so angry with them? I was even mad at Charlie. Well not mad exactly, jealous? He went fishing with Dad. Stop...

"Well girls here we are."

I loved the soft lighting guiding us along the front path of Tully's. It was like walking up to a castle. In the dark, the big trees looked more protective than threatening.

"Thank you so much for walking me home. I thoroughly enjoyed the evening."

Before I knew what was happening I opened my mouth and said, "Is there anything we can do to help you find your family? Anything at all?"

"Hey, that's what I've been thinking," Zoe added quickly.

"Goodness this is so odd, but I was going to say something about that too. There is a powerful stirring in me right now. I have been grieving for years for my lost family. Tonight gave me hope again. Hope there might still be someone here."

Zoe clapped her hands, "Yes, yes, yes! Computers could help. There are ancestry sites. And research sites."

"Oh my, I don't know anything about computers."

"Oh but I do. You might call me a Wiz!" Zoe cocked her head and gave me a little smile. "Okay, Lil? You're only here a few more days, though. I could help all the rest of summer."

Zing, like I won't help at all? Jealous about the music thing?

"I don't have much to go on, though, only a few possessions that have traveled with me through the decades. You two could come over tomorrow and I could show them to you."

"Lil and I are going fishing in the morning. Afternoon okay?"

"Perfect. I'll see you then," Miss Margaret said.

Zoe and I waved goodbye and headed back to Main Street.

"I know we can help her. Don't you?"

"Sure hope so." What had I gotten myself into? A distraction is what, and that was probably a good thing.

Moonlight guided my path as I headed back to the marina. I could see the houseboat, lights still on, welcoming me.

10

LADY ON THE ROCK

Early morning coffee at the Main Street Diner flowed freely. Fishermen, heading out to the lake, took to-go cups with them. The overnight shift workers from the dam stopped in to chat and unwind before heading home.

The harbormaster watched as the sun rose to warm and give life to her earth.

Up early, eager to meet up with her new friend, Zoe did a crazy little dance around her kitchen floor before heading downstairs to the diner.

"Zoe, would you run down to the market stand to get banana squash from Hattie before you and Lillia go fishing this morning?"

"Can't I do it when we get back? Don't want to be late. You say I'm always late. Trying to..."

"You have time. Now off you go."

"You wanted me to do the tables before I go."

"I'll finish up the tables. You run along and get the squash for me."

Grabbing the cash from her mom's hand, Zoe headed off for Hattie's.

Woo-hoo...today would be fun. Zoe smiled, thinking about Mom letting her take out the fishing boat and having a new friend to do it with.

Big, bold sunflowers stood tall in a deep bucket at the front of the market. Hattie looked up from her work of tying small bundles of a sweet smelling green herb.

"Morning Zoe. What's your Mom need?"

"Banana squash ma'am."

"You girls get Miss Margaret home in one-piece last night?"

Handing over the money, Zoe sniffed the fresh peaches in the small paper bags on the counter. "Yes, we sure did. Lil and I are going fishing today. I'm taking her out on my own. Mom said I can use the boat."

"Well isn't that nice? Why not take a couple of those peaches with? My treat."

"Sweet...I mean thanks. See you later."

Squash in one hand, bag of peaches in the other, Zoe hurried back to the diner.

"Hey, Mr. Pottle. Top o'the morning to you. Maybe my friend and I will try some of your special Triple Ripple later."

"Well hello, there Zoe. Say hi to your Mom for me and enjoy your day."

"Will do."

The creepy old man was unlocking the front door of the clock shop. What a weirdo Zoe thought. He gives me the creeps. She hurried into the diner. Squash on the counter. Change plopped next to it. Check and check.

"Thanks, honey. You girls be careful out there. Life vests on at all times. Be sure to take your phone in case you have trouble with the motor or anything. Wagon is outside the..."

"Sure Mom. We'll be fine. See you later." Back through the open door. Smooth, it didn't even get a chance to close. Summer fun ahead.

There it was...the red wagon with poles, vests, bait, snacks...waiting to be whisked off for fishing with a friend.

She yanked her long braid through the back of her Kentucky Wildcats baseball hat and pulled it lower on her head before grabbing the wagon handle. Her flips flops started singing a rhythmic clip-clop, the perfect summer sound, as she headed to the marina.

Lil waited by the houseboat in T-shirt, shorts, and a bright orange visor. She was laughing. What the...? "Hey, what's so funny?" Zoe asked.

"Sorry, you make quite a sight. That wagon is way too little for you."

"Ah. I get it, you laugh at tall Zoe. This is hard work, my small friend. Stooping. Bending. Pulling OUR gear, may I add? Do I wish the handle was about six inches longer? Or I was six inches shorter? But why worry, when I can bend?"

"Good attitude Zoe," Nora said as she stepped out the boat's door. "A little accommodation can avoid a lot of frustration in many a situation."

"Yes indeedy. Ready to go? Sooner we get out and look, more beauties we hook."

Zoe navigated the small boat along the shoreline. "Lookin' for a spot Mom found us last week." She slowed, steering the boat this way and that. "Hmm? Looks like right about here," she said as she killed the motor. "Lil, can you help with the anchor?"

Lillia started slowly letting the anchor slip over the side of the boat.

"Worms are in this pail. Good with putting them on the hook? You're not a sissy city gal are you?"

"Hey...watch who you're calling a sissy. May not be as good as you but I can hook this wiggly worm just fine," Lillia said. Her voice trailed off as she added, "Dad takes me and Charlie fishing a lot, but this time my brother got to go alone with him."

Zoe thought Lil was bummed about not going with her Dad. Well darn it all, we'll do our own fishing and she will have fun! Hooks baited. Lines in the water. Wait.

Zoe's thoughts drifted. A nibble...lost it. "Oops, that was so close."

"Well at least you've had a nibble," Lillia said making an exaggerated sad face.

Zoe wove a fresh worm onto the hook and plopped her line back in the water. "Your turn will come."

"I sure hope your..." Lillia started to say, but then shouted, "Think I might have one!"

"Woo-hoo! Don't lose it. Net is ready and waiting."

Zoe saw Lil was doing it right. Up, down, reel, up, down, reel. Each time she brought the fish closer. She's done this before. Not bad. Not bad at all.

Zoe shifted to get in a better position to net the catch. The boat rocked and rolled, startling Lillia. Nice going dummy, dump her in the lake before she gets her catch, Zoe thought, but Lillia landed the fish.

A quick fist bump as Zoe said, "Way to go city girl. Let's throw it back in OK? I do not eat fish, just catch them."

"Fine with me."

The fish squirmed in Lillia's hands as she took the hook out of its mouth and leaned over the edge of the boat to release it. Sitting upright quickly, her eyes frantically scanned the other shore.

"What is it?"

"Not sure...think I saw someone over there."

Zoe put her hand up to shade her eyes from the strong overhead sun. "Don't see anyone. See shoreline, birds wading. See trees, clouds."

"There, on that rock, a woman in a long white dress, wearing some kind of hat, like an old-fashioned bonnet. Now she's even waving at us."

"Where Lil?"

"There, right there on the rock with the flat top," Lillia said, pointing with the finger of one hand and waving with the other. "It looks like she's trying hard to get our attention. Like she needs help."

"See the rock, but there's no one on it."

"Zoe look, she's so close to the edge. Hey lady be careful, you'll fall!" Lillia spun around and grabbed Zoe's arm.

"Ouch! Let go," Zoe snapped, but the clutching hand stayed.

"It looks like she's trying to get help. She's so close to falling in and we're sitting here doing nothing!"

"Hey, you're hurting me. Let go right now. Are you crazy?" Zoe yanked at Lil's hand, pulling it off. The boat tipped and then righted itself.

"No. No. There is someone there. Look again. I'm sure you'll see her. Pull up anchor. She needs us!" Lil started frantically searching for the anchor line.

"No! Stop Lillia! There is no one there."

11

LILLIA

I snapped at Zoe again, "There is someone there!"

She held her hand up as if I was a little kid and told me, "Whoa, relax! Take a breath. I'll take us over there. Okay? Chill Lil, you're freaking me out."

Finally, I had her convinced. I spun in my seat and started to pull the anchor in over the edge of the boat while the line jumbled in a tangle at my feet. When I looked back up, she was gone. The rope started sliding slowly back through my grip, the anchor lowering into the dark blackness of the lake.

Oh no, where did she go? Did she fall? She needed me to help her. I was sure of it.

Then I realized Zoe was saying something. "Lil, come on, finish up with the anchor so I can take you over to the rock. The rock with no lady on it may I add"

"Never mind," I said. "She's gone."

"Did she fall? Not! Never there," Zoe said under her breath.

"Maybe she just...?"

"Wrongo. She was not there Lil. A nothing can't fall."

I felt myself deflating. With a long exhale of air, I said, "You didn't see her?"

"Well now. Let me think. Hmmm? Nope...did not see her. One last time. There was no one standing on that dang flat-topped rock!"

What was going on? It didn't feel like one of my imaginings. Not this time. Just fishing. Then bam there she was. I got so freaked. No warning vibes or hints something was going to happen.

"Sorry Zoe."

"No problemo, these claw marks on my arm shouldn't scar. What was all that? All that crazy yelling and stuff."

I don't know what to say. Zoe waited for me to speak. I cannot get my thoughts to focus. Think Lillia. If it was an imagining, things changed this time...different.

My insides said someone needed help. Grauntie said it is good to go with your intuition. Your instinct. Your sense. What if your senses are wrong? What if your senses are stupid? What if your senses lie?

I had grown so careful about my reaction to imaginings. I know I see things other people cannot. I have learned to keep quiet about it. I don't like losing control like this. It made me exposed.

"Lil...earth to Lillia."

"Phew, sorry about that Zoe. Guess the sun beating down made me light headed?"

"Or the wild and crazy first catch feeling went to your head?"

"Yeah." I faked a chuckle. "Or the waves rocking the boat hypnotized me."

"And allowed you to travel deep...deep...deep into your mind, to see what was hidden..."

"So I could turn my eyes outward with new powerful vision..."

"Extrasensory vision, to see what others cannot..."

"...with their mere normal human eyes."

"Yes, they with simple eyes do not possess the power of Lil's vision..."

I started feeling this was getting too close to my hidden reality, so I quickly wrapped it up. "And so I saw a lady ghost on a rock."

"Flat-topped rock. Not any old round rock. A full blown, giant boulder with a flat top. Best kind of place for ghosts to stand and wave."

"Really Zoe? Do ghosts need a place to stand? Don't they float around and go through things? Silly girl."

"You are right again oh wise one."

Wanting to keep her even further from the truth, I rubbed circles on my temples with my fingers. "Ah, it is all fading. Back to reality."

"At least the rock is real. And Lil, more I think about it,

she might be real too. She might still be there. Just doesn't want to be seen right this second," Zoe said.

Wait...thought I had her fooled. "Come on, don't get all squirrely on me."

"It's not squirrely to believe in things you can't see. People like me can't see..."

"...with their mere human eyes?"

"Right. No special eyes. No special ears either. You are the special one I guess."

Was she still kidding around? That had a little bite to it.

Zoe quickly switched gears and said, "Hey, did you eat anything today? My Mom always says our body needs fuel. Were you mixed up because you were hungry? I'm sure getting hungry. Let's break open the lunch bags."

"Sounds good to me."

A simple peanut butter and jelly sandwich never tasted so good. The peaches from Hattie were sweet and juicy.

I started feeling better. I needed to think about this. The flat-top rock was only a rock after all. Maybe Zoe was right. We had been out in the sun a long time and I was hungry.

Peering over the top of the water bottle I was sipping from, I saw the rock flicker, on and off, like a bad TV signal.

12

WIZARD'S WORK

"Wanna head up to Pottle's for ice cream later?" Lillia asked as Zoe motored back to the marina.

"Absolutely positively yes. Or should we head up to Miss Margaret's first? Remember we were going to meet her today?" Zoe threw the rope over the piling and then gathered up the gear, putting it back in the wagon.

"That's right."

Zoe thought about how Lil had laughed and kidded around about what happened on the lake. She is keeping something hidden. Trying to get more out of her, Zoe said, "I was thinking, could be that all that stuff today has a connection with last night."

"Last night?"

"You two thought the music might be coming from the flat-top rock area, right? And you saw something on the rock today, right again?"

"Well, that second part I'm not so sure of anymore."

Zoe shrugged and called it as she saw it. "Now I think you're lying. At least admit you saw something."

"That's a rotten thing to say."

Zoe stared straight ahead.

Lillia's face flushed and her mouth tightened.

Zoe waited a few more seconds before saying, "Well?"

"Okay, I did see something. But it could have been the light bouncing funny or a shadow...."

Zoe could not believe what Lil was saying. Couldn't she say yes without muddling her answer up? Black or white...yes or no... saw or didn't see?

Lillia sped up her pace, separating the two. Zoe lagged behind pulling the wagon. Well huff and puff Lil, act all upset. Say you want to help Miss Margaret, but I think not. You won't even face the possibility that the rock could be a clue. Get real Lil.

Zoe dropped the wagon outside the diner. Ahead Lil was waiting on Pottle's bench. Zoe walked by her, giving a come-on-along wave of her hand as she passed.

Miss Margaret waited on the front porch swing. "Good morning girls. I'm so excited to see you. I could barely sleep last night. How was the fishing?"

"It was great. This one did all right for a city girl."

"Oh gee thanks, Zoe. Make's me so happy to know I meet with your approval."

Zoe didn't see the punch coming. Ouch! That was hard. "Good swing for a city girl too."

"Now girls...sparring again? If you two can manage to behave, I would like to take you up to my apartment. I have a few things I want to show you." As Miss Margaret opened the gigantic front door, its colored glass panel threw off sparkles that bounced around the entry hall. "Walk quietly so we don't disturb anyone else."

Light fled with the closing of the door. Ahead was a staircase with worn floral carpet. The handrail was so wide the girls' fingers could not reach around it.

"I wanna slide down this later. Sure, could get up speed on this baby!" Zoe exclaimed.

"Oh, my. I do not believe my housemates would approve. They scolded me when I tried it."

Lillia stopped on the third step. "You tried it?"

Miss Margaret kept walking, stepping around her. "Well, just that once. Come along now girls."

Zoe's what's-up-with-that look made Lillia giggle. Then Miss Margaret burst out laughing. "Oh goodness no, I was kidding. But, when I was your age, you can bet I would have tried it."

She unlocked the door to her small apartment. It was neat and tidy, like her. It had a little old lady smell, powdery and clean. She plumped a pillow in the corner of the couch and motioned the girls to sit. Lillia and Zoe sat one on each end of the couch.

"Now girls, you know some of the story about me I suspect. My parents died when I was young. I was adopted by a distant relative and taken far away. Most of what I remember was my life away from this area. I had a good life, but in my heart, there was always a sense of something missing."

"Oh, that must have been hard. So you missed your old home? I miss my old home sometimes too. But gotta look forward Mom says. So I do."

"Daring to look ahead is what I am about to do Zoe. Do you girls know the meaning of serendipitous events?"

"Like lucky ones?"

"Right. Serendipitous means finding something good without looking for it, by chance, by accident. I think serendipity was a stir in my universe yesterday. I have a strong sense Lillia and I being together at that one special moment in the moonlight, was why I could hear the music. And when you two offered to help me find my family, well I found myself thinking why not give it a go? So I want to show you a few possessions hoping they might be clues." She turned to walk into the bedroom.

Zoe gave a sniff, raised her eyebrows and said, "The music coming from the rock across the lake? Why just today Lillia saw..." Zoe dragged out the words, turning to glance at Lillia who was gritting her teeth and giving small shakes of her clenched fist.

She returned to the room carrying a box and set it down. Rectangular and covered in a faded rose print; its worn edges showed it had been around a long time...like her.

"What was that you were saying Zoe?"

"Nothing, right Lillia? Let's check out your stuff."

She carefully started to remove the lid and then paused again to say, "I want last night to be more than a momentary dance in the moonlight. I feel there must be someone here in White Cliff Landing who remembers the little Margaret from long ago. And I want to find that person so very badly."

Then Miss Margaret took the top of the box off and we looked inside.

13

LILLIA

I woke to the sound of raindrops rattling on the ceiling over my head. Do not open your eyes. Pretend you are in your own bed at home upstairs under the eaves. The raindrops are falling on the roof...the trees...the fence...the fields all around.

Tucker loves the rain and would be waiting at the door to run out and get wet. Mom would patiently wipe his muddy paws off when he came back in.

Odors from brewing coffee. My cat Sam curling up at the foot of Mom's kitchen stool. The cupboards a soft white against the pale buttery yellow walls and tan tile floor. Strawberry jam waiting for me to spread on my toast. A small glistening glass of orange juice sitting to the right.

Charlie waking in the next room. He would want to turn on cartoons as soon as he popped into the kitchen.

Mom would say, "No way Jose, breakfast and teeth brushing first."

Keeping my eyes closed, I could almost hear Dad's goodbyes to Mom before he headed to work and her low laugh as she gave him one of her big hugs.

I was good at pretending.

Opened my eyes...ceiling inches above me. Ah, well Toto...not in Kansas anymore.

I tightened my neck muscles to raise my head and shoulders and peer out the small round window. Oh terrific, a cheery summer rain.

Rolling onto my tummy, I dropped my feet over the side of the bed. Twisting them around to find the first step of the ladder, I climbed down out of my bunk.

TV tuned to a morning news program. Now I smelled real coffee.

Grauntie sat at a table reading the newspaper and sipping coffee from her big white mug. She had her reading glasses perched on her nose and her hair pinned up in the usual haphazard way. She was wearing faded jeans and a T-shirt from our Grand Canyon adventure. That sure was a fun one. Charlie and I loved hiking the trails curling around the canyon cliffs. Grauntie would tell us to hug the inside wall and not look down.

"Good morning sleepy head."

"Morning."

The chair teetered beneath me as I sat down, propping

my elbows on the table's edge and propping my chin in my palm. "Grauntie?"

"Yes, sweetie."

"You talk to Mom and Dad. Do you know why Mom was so squirrely this week? It was like she couldn't wait 'til I was gone."

Pushing her reading glasses up to the top of her head, she looked me directly. "Oh my, all these questions so early in the morning. Thought you'd be asking about the wonderful aroma coming from the oven."

Her eyes shifted away and she got up from her seat. "Far as I know your mom is fine."

She moved to take the rolls out of the oven. "Okay sweetie, how about enjoying these rolls now? Zoe will be here soon and we can start our trip to the LBL."

Ah, yes Zoe. Wish I could get out this trip with her. The butter slid off my knife and onto the swirls of the warm roll. "Maybe we shouldn't go. It's raining, might get worse."

Grauntie Nora came up behind me and kissed the top of my head. "Lillia, aren't you happy to have this time together with me?"

"You know I love being with you. Feel bad you ended up inviting Zoe. Sort of wish it was just the two of us."

"Well, I'm glad she's coming along. We would not get much exploring in if it was only the two of us. I can't keep up with you like I used to."

I decided I would not be such a Debbie Downer.

Neither Zoe pushing my buttons, nor Mom being afraid of me, are Grauntie's problems.

Across the room, on a bookcase, were some of the family photos that always traveled with her. There was one of Charlie as a baby, curled up against Tucker. Mom, with Dad's arm around her, sitting on a picnic table. They had big smiles and their eyes squinted in the sunshine. In my photograph I was swinging on the rope swing in our back-yard, laughing up at the sky, my legs reaching up to pump myself higher.

In the row of windows above the bookcase, the first rays of sunshine were peeking out from the clouds. Looked like the rain was over.

14

LEAVING THE HARBOR

The morning sun broke through the low-hanging clouds. Moist ozone laden air invigorated the village residents, grateful for the temporary suspension of the summer heat and dryness.

Peter whistled as he erased Triple Ripple and replaced it with Double Trouble Chocolate on his outdoor sign.

The clock man was having his morning coffee alone at his small table. Last night he had dreamt a familiar dream of traveling on a ship, roaming strange worlds, tossed on wild seas by the powerful winds of a relentless thunderstorm. Not being able to find his way back home.

Hattie had freshly stocked her farm stand for the day and dropped off fruit and vegetables with Nora for her overnight trip to LBL.

Julia made sure Zoe packed her toothbrush and a fresh

change of clothes before they walked the bikes down the hill to the houseboat.

The harbormaster watched as the older woman navigated Lady of the Lake out of the harbor. He silently wished them smooth passage to the other side and safe travels on the land. It was a big lonely land, emptied of human life decades ago.

On the upper deck, with the wind in their faces, Zoe and Lillia watched as the LBL got closer.

Zoe said, "Your grandaunt is way cool. This trip is going to be sweet."

"Yep, she is. Zoe, did you mean what you said yesterday?"

"That you're a liar?"

"Yeah, that."

"I did mean it. Not good to lie, especially to yourself. Thought you wanted to help Miss Margaret find her family?"

"I do want to help her. I want us both to help her."

"Talk is cheap. Know I am going to do everything I can. Are you?"

"Of course, I am. Why do you even say that?"

"Should have told her what you saw. She is thinking you are special. That you helped her hear the music. Pretty low not to tell her about seeing the lady on the music rock."

"Well, I wasn't sure...."

"Oh okay, that again. Whatever Lil. Just wish we were

partners in this. I'm going to really put in an effort. You, I'm not so sure about."

15

LILLIA

I couldn't figure out why Zoe was getting so snarky. I'm going to work hard too. She had no right to say that. Who did she think she was? Oh, now I remember...a Wiz. Well la-di-da.

"There's the flat-topped rock. Are you getting any sort of vibe from it?" Zoe asked.

"Nope, not a thing. No lady, no music."

"Are you sure?"

"Would it matter what I said? You called me a lazy liar."

"And special, don't forget that," Zoe said, grinning and reaching around to stick her face in mine.

Why was she smiling? Nothing amusing in her chatter. I could pretend I was seasick and get Grauntie to turn the boat back.

Zoe turned her face toward the shore and the rock

again. "Sorry Lil. Might be that I'm a little jealous. I think it's pretty cool, to be honest."

"What's cool? Acting crazy or seeing things? You calling me a liar?"

"I said I was sorry. Wish I had something special. Wish I was good luck like Miss Margaret thinks you are. Mom says don't count on luck to get good grades, you have to work for them. So Lil, luck and chance...good for you. I, however, am going to have to work if we want to find her family. Like, learn about the history around here. Find old records. Like a birth certificate."

I was not sure what to make about the whole serendipity thing. Sure I heard the music...I should say, we heard the music. So not an imagining then? Dad said I shouldn't believe in my imaginings, that they're just make-believe. But maybe I should? Argh...my thinker was hurting again.

I said, "There is a ton of work to do. And I'm going to do everything I can."

Zoe didn't let it drop. She started in on the rock again. "We're closer now. Anything unusual? Be honest with me."

"Nope, nada."

"Hmmm, doesn't mean there wasn't something there, now does it? Music? A lady? Keep your mind open. Mine always is. Be ready for any possibilities."

That's what Grauntie always says too. Easy to say. I think more about closing some of the circuits, so they don't get me in trouble again. And I will be keeping my mouth shut. Hurts to be called a liar.

Zoe and I both were in a better mood after watching Grauntie Nora try to dock in an overnight slip.

She was so funny. Back and forth we went. She would navigate in and then decide she was too far from the dock. Then with a big hoot, she would pull back out. "Oh well, try again." So she tried again. Meanwhile, Zoe and I were cracking up.

"Ah my little ones, I'm happy to be able to offer such amusement to you."

"Sorry, it's just that..."

"No apologies please," she said, as she too burst out laughing. "We all have to laugh, especially at ourselves. It's good for our souls." She threw the lines over the pilings. "And makes life a whole lot easier."

We unloaded the bikes.

"Okay, girls off you go. Be sure to pay attention to your path so you can find your way back."

Zoe said, "I have my cell phone along. Dang, no signal bars. Well, I'll take it along anyway. Never know. I can take photos with it."

"Great idea. We might see something to share with Miss Margaret," I said.

"Stick together girls. See you later."

"Bye Grauntie. Love you."

"Love you too sweetie."

16

GOLDEN POND

The sky was cloudless and the air was still. With soft gentle curves, the narrow paved road took the two bike riders through forests and across expansive valleys. Up hills to see beautiful vistas, and down again they went. Sun on their faces and wind in their hair.

It was a beautiful land. Sunshine dappled the forested areas with yellow filtered light. In the open fields, the insects flew their disjointed dance among the prairie grasses and flowers.

Cresting a small hill, Zoe stopped to point out a small herd of bison resting in the shade of a grove of trees in the distance. "Aren't they cool Lillia? Mom said they were almost all killed off at one time. So many hunters I guess. Government brought a few back in. Now look at the size of the herd. Pretty neat, huh? Wouldn't want to meet one up close."

"Me either. They sure are big."

"I rode a horse once and it was huge but so sweet. These guys, not so much. Big heads and horns. Kind of rough and tough."

Lillia said, "It would be awesome to try to ride one, though...their coats look so soft and thick. Can't you imagine hanging on to that big furry neck, laying low against it? Galloping across those hills?"

"I'll take a horse any day."

They found the sign for the Golden Pond Visitor Center and turned their bikes in toward the parking lot. A few tourists were wandering around inside the center as the girls entered.

"This place has tons of displays about LBL. History and stuff. Love imagining what life must have been like. No computer, no TV, no cell phones," Zoe said.

"How about no phones at all?"

Zoe smacked herself upside her head and said, "Right, duh...oh my gosh, talk about impossible to imagine."

The first section they came to showed a history of the Native American Indian tribes who had lived in this area of Kentucky. How they hunted, cleared land for agriculture and settled into permanent villages.

Lillia read the sign next to a map of Kentucky showing where tribes had lived. "The origins of the name Kentucky may have come from a Native American word Kah-ten-tahte meaning Land of Tomorrow. Another possible meaning for Kentucky was dark and bloody ground, referring to the violent ancient tribal confrontations that occurred here."

"Yuck, who would name a state after something so gross?" Zoe said. She stepped to the next display. "Hey Lillia, doesn't this look like your flat-top rock?"

"You know it does. Pretty cool costumes the Indians are wearing." Lillia read the diorama description. "These Indians are dressed in formal, ceremonial garb. Intricate beading represents figures from the spirit world. The large rock, with its distinctive flat top, was a sacred site for the Native Americans. Here they performed traditional cere-monies, believing it to be a portal for spirits to travel through, crossing between this earth and the spirit world."

"Holy schmoly! Do you believe that? Might explain the lady and the music. A portal. An entryway. To where and from where?"

Lillia stood staring at the scene behind the window. "Do you believe the rock is a special place?"

Zoe thought a moment before answering. "You know Lil, maybe the lady in the bonnet was like a spirit from another time. She came through this rock, or on it, or what-ever. Only you were able to see her. Or maybe it's a pathway for people like you..."

"Hey, what do you mean...like me?"

"You have some special ability...aren't like us normal kids."

"That is a crazy idea," Lillia said. "What makes you think you are any more normal than me? Huh?"

"Ouch...my little friend has some spunk. Well, it looks like the Indians used it for help...so why not you? And heck what do we know?" Zoe snapped a couple of photos. "My hairbrush could be a portal."

Zoe grinned, shrugged, and walked to another display. "Hey come over here Lil, look at this photo. A whole house moved across the lake. How'd they do that? Says they put the house on a barge. Smarge barge...I can't imagine moving a house."

"Wow. Listen to this, 'Entire villages, general stores, churches and post offices were moved or demolished when the Land Between the Lakes was made into a recreational area.' Hard to believe."

"But it was still gonna be their home right? Only in a different place? Is your house your home, or is your home your house?" Zoe asked.

"Do you girls have any questions?"

Startled, Zoe and Lillia turned to see a tall gray-haired woman standing directly behind them. Her disapproving eyes stared at them through wire-rimmed glasses. Her arms tightly crossed against her chest. Her thin lips tilted downward.

"Ah, no, I don't think so," Lillia said.

Zoe spoke up and asked for a map of the LBL.

"What type of map do you want? We have road maps, hiking maps, graveyard maps, and historical maps."

"Road and hiking maps, please," Zoe said.

"Aren't you a little young to be here by yourself?"

"We are here with family."

"Very well, come along and I'll find the map you need."

"Zoe, what are graveyard maps?" Lillia whispered.

"Not sure, should we ask her?"

Lillia nodded.

"Ma'am, could you please tell us what the graveyard maps are for?"

"Not for children," she replied sharply. "There are over two hundred sacred family burial grounds scattered across LBL. They are to be respected and not treated like tourist sites."

The girls decided they had better not ask for one of those maps. With a quick thank you, they left Golden Pond Visitor Center.

17

LILLIA

I saw the girl approaching us as we unlocked our bikes.

She had the strangest eyes. Pale green. Really, really pale green. Made me think of the pictures of the Luna moth my science teacher had shown us. Cute hair cropped short with sunny streaks in it.

"Excuse me, but I couldn't help overhearing you ask about the graveyards."

"Yeah, what was with that person? You'd think we were asking to have a seance in the graveyards," Zoe said.

"She's protective of the family cemeteries. She doesn't want tourists trampling all over them. I could show you one of them. I know where most of them are," the green-eyed girl said.

"Oh cool. Sorry, not cool, bad way to put it. What's a family cemetery? Don't know if I want to see one, though.

Are they creepy with all those dead people? I've never been to one. How about you Lil?" Zoe asked.

"My Grandpa used to take me to visit a cemetery."

* * *

The memories of that place came tumbling in. The headstones stood in orderly rows. Flowers placed in metal vases mounted to the stones. Grass trimmed to a sharp crispness. The letters in the gravestones etched deep into the surface.

During those visits, Grandpa talked to me about the importance of respecting the dead. We talked about Charlie's twin and visited her grave.

I asked Grandpa "So if Chloe was never born, did I ever have a little sister?"

"Of course, you did Lillia. She was alive, but not long enough to be born into this world," Grandpa answered. "There are dimensions of life and planes of existence that most people cannot imagine."

"I don't get that at all Grandpa."

"Dimension is a size or space. Life is a force, an energy. A very wise man once said, energy cannot be destroyed. It just changes form. So there are spaces where the energy goes that we do not know understand. Places we humans can't go."

"You're scaring me."

"Oh my sweet little Lillia, do not be afraid. Think of the wonderful possibilities!" He swept his arms out and starting spinning around.

I started laughing. "The possibility you'll fall?"

He stopped and bent over with laughter. "Good one Lillia."

"But really Grandpa. I don't get what you mean."

He gave me a hug and said we could talk more later.

He passed away soon after that day. I have often wondered what he would have told me.

Grauntie said he looked a lot like me. Did he have imaginings too? Was he laughed at? Did he understand what was happening to him? Could he have helped me? Questions I will never get answers to, so why not put them far away in the back corners of my mind?

* * *

"Lil? Lillia Pameroy? Ready to head out? Home Place? Emily here said she'd meet us tomorrow to show us a cemetery."

"All right with you?" Emily asked me.

"We'll probably be leaving to go back to White Cliff Landing tomorrow. I don't think it'll work out, but thanks."

"In case you change your mind, I'll be waiting for you by the flat-top rock."

Her words hung in the air. Before I could say anything more, she got on her rusty old bike and rode off.

Zoe asked, "Why'd you brush Emily off? I think it would be neat to visit one of those cemeteries. The whole thing about meeting her by the rock, wowza! To be right by that...what they call it? Portal? You're not scared are you? Might be a clue. You said you'd work hard. Of all the places she could meet us, right? Curious. Serendip...whatever that word was."

"Serendipitous and stop it. I am not scared. Just thought she was odd."

"Well, I don't think she's odd. Seemed nice," Zoe answered.

I didn't want to argue with her. "Come on let's get going," I said as I threw my leg over the center of the bike and pushed off with a strong pedal.

18

THE HOME PLACE

The Home Place gift shop was busy with people who had arrived on a tour bus.

"Hi, y'all. I'm Delcie. Welcome to the Home Place. Here you will experience what life was like in the past. Our farm family members, dressed in period costume, welcome questions regarding this living farm. They can tell you what chores they do, how the animals are cared for, and such. Please feel free to ask any question you might have."

Zoe and Lillia paid the admittance fee, pushed through the turnstile, and started down the rambling path leading to the gray weathered home. Stalks of cut corn formed upright teepees, parading on the field next to it. A fence of rough-hewn timbers did a crisscross dance along the path's side. Soft field grasses swayed, bending and rising, in the afternoon breeze.

Ladies in sunbonnets and long full-skirted dresses

worked in the garden. On an outside clothesline, drying garments fluttered in the wind. A young girl with a handled basket over her arm, tossed corn kernels out to feed the chickens. She smiled and waved to the girls as they passed.

Men sat on simple three legged stools as they worked, repairing equipment. Cattle stood in a pasture, grazing on the grass.

The farmhouse was actually two structures under one roof, separated by a breezeway. A porch spanned the entire length and wrapped around on one side.

In the open area between the two parts of the house sat a woman in costume, mending what looked like a child's shirt. Next to her feet was a black cat sunning itself.

"Welcome. Our home is built in the dogtrot style. In this breezeway, my family can sit on a hot day and try to catch a cool breeze passing through. We use daylight to work here and still be out of the sun's rays or protected from the rain. Please take a tour of our home."

She pointed to her left. "That side is where my family gathers to prepare and eat their meals. On the other side are a sitting area and sleeping quarters. Downstairs is the master bedroom and upstairs is the children's bedroom."

The tour group had made their way to the log farmhouse.

Zoe nudged Lillia and said, "Hey Lil, want to head over to the barn, or go see those cute little lambs by the fence over there first? The house will be so crowded now." She started down the steps from the porch.

"Sure, good idea I guess," Lillia said hurrying to catch up with Zoe.

"Look at the log buildings. This is pretty cool huh? I was here once before. Wouldn't it be fun to work here? Wear costumes and get to talk to people all day?"

"Sounds like a perfect job for you," Lillia said. "Getting to talk all day!"

19

LILLIA

I loved this place. I had never seen anything like it. Stepping back into a long-ago time felt good, felt familiar somehow.

The sounds of the animals echoed and bounced around in my head. A voice interrupted my thoughts..."Oh, sorry Zoe. What were you saying?"

Small lambs frolicked among the larger sheep. Zoe had stopped to step up on the fence rail and reach across to pet them. "I said, I'm going to take photos of those lambs. I'll catch up with you."

"Okay."

Ahead I saw the barn. I liked old places. I liked to imagine what had happened in them. Think about the people who had lived and worked in them.

In the dark interior, I could make out horses in stalls. Their tails lazily swished away flies. Seated on a small bench, cut in half by the door shadow, a man repaired a harness.

Grauntie always said places were alive with their histories. Fragments of life energies left behind. Memories absorbed. She made places sound alive...almost human. What stories the walls could tell if only someone had the right ears. Slow down once in a while, listen. You will hear what they are saying.

Okay, Grauntie. Here goes. Let me see if I can hear the stories. I touched the barn door handle and felt a slight vibration. Shimmery sunbeams. Shafts of light. Musty animal scents. Earthy odors. Dry brittle oldness.

You can hear the stories

I yanked my hand away and spun quickly to look for the speaker. Not Zoe, she was still standing on the fence. Not the farmer, he was still bent over his work.

Lady still on the porch talking to the tour group. Black cat still there sunning itself, stretching its neck as a young girl bent to pet it. The girl stood up and looked at me.

The girl with the green eyes.

Words flooded my brain and sloshed up against my skull. I felt light headed. The words started forming together...

You know how to listen and hear things
You know how to look and see things
You know how to touch and feel things
Old things
Unsettled things
Be still
Be open

"Lil, what's wrong? Did you see a ghost? Jeez, you're scaring me. What's going on? Talk to me." Zoe was shaking my shoulders. "Snap out of it."

"Hey, easy. I'm all right."

Am I? What was all that? Who was talking inside my head? The barn? The girl?

"You go ahead. I'll be up shortly. I need to...ah...pet a lamb." Please just go away, Zoe. I don't want your negative vibes now. I don't want to answer your stupid questions. Sometimes I don't know things and everything isn't black and white.

"Fine, I'll pet it again too."

"No Zoe, please go back to the house. I'll be right there."

"All right, all right. I'm going, but if you're not there..."

"Go."

20

THE PHOTOGRAPH

Zoe stepped up onto the porch and said hello to the young costumed girl petting the cat. She turned, crossing her arms over her chest, and watched as Lil stood by the barn door. She sure was acting weird again. This gal might have a screw loose. Zoe figured she would park her butt right here on this bench and keep an eye on her.

After a few minutes, Zoe saw Lil start walking up toward the house. Hmmm, good, she's headed this way.

Lillia held up her hand, fending off any questions from Zoe. "No questions. Let's tour this house now."

"All right, but I want to talk later. You are not telling me something. I just know it." Zoe walked behind Lil and noticed how intently she looked at the girl and the cat. What is going on?

"Hello, there young ladies. Glad to see you came back

to tour our home," the farm lady said. "The children's sleeping area is right up that staircase."

Lillia and Zoe climbed the steps to the upper floor and found the children's room under the steeply sloped roof. Old wooden toys arranged on the rug as though a young child had just left the room.

Zoe walked to the far corner, ducking her head under the eaves to see a cradle in the corner. "Glad there's no baby doll in here. Never cared for dolls. They creep me out. Like there's something alive inside of them."

"Lots of stuff creeps you out."

"Maybe, smarty, but remember the Chucky movie? You have to admit that was some major scary. Dolls hold spirits inside. They give me the heebie-jeebies," Zoe said as she spun on her heel and headed to leave. "Come on, it's hot and stuffy up here."

A long table, with a mix match of wooden chairs, practically took over the entire kitchen. Rag rugs softened the worn plank floor. A cast iron cooking stove against the back wall.

"This is the main gathering room for our family after chores are finished. The cook stove is used to heat the room and to dry the laundry hung in here during the cold winter months. I am churning the cream from our cow's milk into butter."

"Can you imagine...not even a microwave?" Zoe whispered.

"And no refrigerator...eew."

"Didn't need a can opener either I guess."

"And clearing the table didn't mean loading the dishwasher."

"You got that right. Come on Lil, let's go across to the other side now."

Crossing through the breezeway the girls entered the parlor, a room that had served as both a family gathering place as well as a bedroom for the parents. A small settee, two side chairs, and a rocker faced the fireplace. In the corner was a chest of drawers with a crocheted dresser scarf and a bed.

A counted cross-stitch piece hung above the dresser with a floral design and the verse, 'A man's work is from sun to sun, but a mother's work is never done.'

"Hey, my mom would love that one. Gonna try to remember it," Zoe said.

Hanging nearby, on the same wall, was an old framed photograph.

21

LILLIA

I stared at the framed photograph.

The description read, 'Four generations of the Pottle and Hellerman families gather for a reunion at their family farm.'

It showed a group of people on what looked to be the porch of this house. They stared straight out at a camera that must have been set up on the lawn.

Zoe was questioning the woman about the quote. A group of tourists oohed and aahed over a clock on the fireplace mantle as it chimed the hour.

I wondered if any of the people in the photo were related to Peter Pottle? I was turning away when one figure in the group caught my eye. A lady in a sunbonnet, holding the hand of a little girl. Her other arm wrapped around the elbow of a tall young man next to her. From under her long skirt, the tip of her shoe peeked out.

It moved.

What...?

More motion. Subtle. Behind the glass. Blink of an eye...glance shifted...wisp of hair lifted by the wind.

It was the woman in the white dress. She had come to me again.

She released the child's hand and her arm left the young man's elbow. She stepped off the porch and in unhurried liquid movements she started across the lawn...slowly undoing her sunbonnet ties...face growing larger until it filled the photograph...it could not contain her.

Removing her bonnet, she reached to support herself on the frame then passed through the glass, stepped out of the photograph and into the room. The very room I stood in.

Soft warm air passed over me, through me.

You can help me

Detached, weightless, I followed as she walked toward the window. I stood beside her and looked out.

Children played on the grounds...people sat on the porch chatting, laughing...men smoked cigars off to one side...horses tied to hitching posts...dogs ran, barking and playing with the children. Soft words murmured...

Please help my family be together again

...she passed out through the window glass.

I watched her walk down the three porch steps and over to the pathway. Coming up toward her was the green-eyed girl. They embraced and turned to wave at me.

Me, Lillia Pameroy, with my face, pressed against the window glass.

"The lady says the quote..."

I did not want to leave the scene outside the window. Wait. I don't understand. Family?

"...was pretty common. Mom would like it. Memorize quote oh mind of mine." Zoe chattered at me. "Lil? What are you staring at? What's outside?"

Fading, blurring, the scene shifted, bending back to now. The woman and green-eyed girl became a mom and her daughter waving goodbye to friends.

The girl pulled up an old bike from where it had been leaning on the fence. She pushed it along as they walked away. The people on the porch were now the tour group gathered to return to their bus.

"Come on, we better get going. I want to be sure we get to back to the houseboat before dark," Zoe said. "Lil, hey earth to Lillia." Zoe waved her hand in front of my face.

"Yeah sure, before dark," my voice said. Turning back to see the photo, I could see it was over. It still hung on the wall. She was still in it, staring out at the unseen photographer. She smiled as she held her little girl's hand...still frozen in time.

I followed Zoe out to the porch. We walked down the steps and along the path leading back to the main entrance.

On one of the fence posts hung a sunbonnet, tie strings fluttering in the wind.

22

JENNIFER TALKS

Another day was winding down. The Lady of the Lake securely anchored for its overnight stay at Hellerman Marina. The bait shop had closed for the day. The small General Store and Antique Emporium stayed open for those last minute supply runs tourists so often had to make.

The vanishing of daylight was usually a lingering and quieting time of day. Here in the Kentucky hill country, it happened suddenly. The onset of night's darkness was quick and unsympathetic to anyone caught in it.

The road coiled out of the harbor, up a slight rise, and into the darkening forest. Soon to be completely enveloped in dark shadows.

She did not consider herself the worrying type, but Grauntie Nora felt a bit of anxiety creeping in as she waited for the girls' return. Sitting on the top deck of the boat was the best vantage point to watch and wait.

* * *

Nora's mind kept replaying her earlier phone conversation with Jennifer. "How have you been feeling? Adam said the pregnancy morning sickness is bad."

"What else did he tell you? That I'm acting crazy? The bad memories have come a callin'? I'm afraid of my daughter all over again?"

Nora was caught off guard, unsure what to say next. She remembered the awful time eight years ago when Jen and Adam found out Charlie's twin sister had died, even before she had a chance to breathe.

"Jen, you know Lillia had nothing to do with Chloe's death."

"Do I Nora? Do I really? I look at Lillia and don't know what to think. She's the one who told me Chloe was dead."

"Jen, she didn't say that."

"Don't spilt hairs Nora. Not those exact words. My daughter touched my belly and told me the baby was moving. Cute hah? When I asked her if both babies were moving, she said, don't be silly Mommy, dolls don't move. Silly, stupid me tried explaining that there are two babies. She kept saying no Mommy. The doll is not a real baby, she says, all cute and innocent. My god, what normal four-year-old kids say stuff like that?"

"Jen, she was so young and doesn't remember what she said or what happened. She sure doesn't understand why you are so upset with her now."

"Whatever Nora. I remember that's when the horror started for me."

Nora tried distracting her and talked about Lillia's stay so far, trying to keep upbeat and positive.

"I love you, Jen. Our family will get through all this. Do you want me to have Lillia call you later?"

"No, the signal is bad."

"Okay. Get some rest. We'll talk again soon."

* * *

Nora was glad to see the girls riding their bikes out of the darkening forest.

"Welcome back. How was your day exploring?"

"So much fun. We went to the visitor center. The grouchy old woman there told us about family cemeteries. We saw a living farm. Way cool. So different from now. An ancient place," Zoe said.

"Oh, my Zoe...ancient hah? Bet I would remember a few of the things you saw. You're quiet Lillia. How did you like it?"

I told Grauntie about our day, leaving out a few things like the voices in my head. Of course, I left out meeting the woman walking out of the photograph.

"The Home Place was great. It was like a farm in an old story come to life. I loved the characters there and how they made it come alive, like we had stepped back in time."

"Think I'll try to get a job there next summer. Mom said I'm a good actress," Zoe said.

"Zoe, I think you would be perfect at that. You are so at ease talking with people."

Grauntie mentioned Mom called and asked me if I wanted to give her a callback.

"It's kind of late, maybe tomorrow," I mumbled. I do not want to talk to her, afraid I might get mad or homesick.

"Well, I had a good day too. See what I bought at the little antique shop." Grauntie showed us a beautiful clock.

"I thought it would be a nice thank you gift to give Hattie. But it needs a winding key."

"Hey, we saw a clock sort of like that. Right on the mantel at the farmhouse. Bet that creepy clock shop in town would have a key," Zoe said.

"Great suggestion. I'll check that out when we get back. Would you girls like to sleep up top under the stars tonight? You could carry cushions and blankets to the upper deck and make yourselves a night nest."

"Oh, I'd love to! Girl Scout camping trip was last time I slept outside, but it was in a tent. This would be so fun," Zoe said.

After we finished dinner, Grauntie helped us settle in on the upper deck. "You girls sleep tight now. See you in the morning."

Lying on our backs, with our hands clasped behind our heads, we stared up at the smiling man in the moon.

I took a deep breath and let out a big happy sigh.

"We have to ask your grandaunt...wait, I mean grauntie, if we can stop at the rock tomorrow. We just have to. Too many coincidences Lil. The music, the waving person, the portal thingie. And Emily! Can you believe it? She wants to show us a cemetery near the rock. Way too many coincidences."

Please don't start in on all of that again. I want to have some quiet time to think about what happened today. Alone thinking time. "I don't know. I don't think Grauntie can drive the houseboat up to just any shore. Isn't the full moon awesome?"

"Changing the subject? Typical for you. Can't we at least ask?"

"Grauntie's done so much all ready. Anyway, what's her name seemed sort of odd didn't she? Bet she won't even show up," I said.

"Emily. No, not to me. I have pretty good radar as far as odd and crazy people. Like the clock man in town, he's odd to me. That Emily girl didn't even make my radar beep. Now, what was with you today Lil? Something happened and you're not sharing," Zoe said, wagging her finger at me. "You can tell me anything."

Oh sure I thought, and have you call me names? What would you say if I told you Emily isn't a living person?

"I can tell you are holding a lot of stuff in Lil and that is not good."

If only she knew. The few times in my life when I did try saying something, things did not go well. Kids teased and made fun of me, talked behind my back. Adults didn't believe me and questioned my sanity. I learned to keep things to myself.

But did Zoe's questions deserve an answer? Maybe I needed to face the reality of me. "So if I tell you something, you promise you won't laugh? Or call me a liar?"

"I won't laugh. And if you tell me the truth I won't call you a liar."

Sometimes the truth isn't easy to figure out. Sometimes

it is so hard to know what is true. Staring up at the night sky, I thought about how I could explain my imaginings to Zoe. With a deep focusing breath, I began. "You know how when you are little, you play pretend games?"

"Sure, I do."

"And how you have imaginary friends or you make believe you are living in a castle?"

"Sure, I remember."

"Or you think you see a monster under the bed?"

"Sure, I've felt that."

"And how you tell ghost stories around the campfire and make yourself scared?"

"Sure, it was so much fun out in the dark."

"Then when you got older you stopped doing that?"

"That's why we're not kids anymore."

"I still imagine things sometimes."

"You mean like imagining how those snazzy new shoes would look with your jeans? Or imagining the cute guy sitting at the next desk is watching you? Actually, I like those kinds of imaginings."

Lying here, not looking into Zoe's eyes, made the next words come out a little easier. "No, not exactly. More like, ah, not sure how to say this. I see things other people don't."

Zoe popped straight up. She turned to peer down at me. There was enough light from the moon to see her eyes staring at me.

I waited. She did not speak. Guess telling her this wasn't such a good idea.

"Well. You finally admitted it." She laid back down. "So, go on."

"My mom calls them my imaginings. She told me I must have an over active mind. My dad says don't let your imagination run away with you, you're a big girl now."

"So then you really are seeing these things? They are really there?"

"I guess I don't know quite how to answer. I know it feels like I do see the things. Like the lady on the rock, I saw her, but you didn't."

"You're right, I didn't see her. But Lil, that doesn't mean she wasn't real."

"Don't laugh at me, Zoe."

"Hey I'm not laughing, I'm trying to make you realize you're not crazy. Like, if I was blind, I couldn't see you, but you would still be you. Right?"

"So where are you going with this?" I knew Zoe was trying to force me to face what I had been avoiding.

"Well my little friend, it might be that you have another sense. Sight, hearing, touch, taste, smell and, what do you call it?"

"Imagining?"

"Yep...you have an imagining sense!"

24

NIGHT COMES

"Or a stronger sense of sight? Like the dogs that can smell cancer. Their smellers are super powerful. Humans cannot do that. Maybe my sight sense is somehow different?"

Zoe gasped, "Or maybe," her voice lowered, "You have the sixth sense."

"What's that?"

"ESP," Zoe whispered. "Extrasensory perception. OMG, that would be way cool. Talk to spirits and tell the future. Think about that."

"I don't know if I want to. I'm feeling pretty odd already."

"Does it hurt you? Like, give you a headache or something?"

"No."

"Let's think about this. You have to learn to work with

this. Let us call it a talent. I could help you. We could solve people's problems. Or help someone talk to a relative who died. Or, like if someone lost their dog, we could help them find her. Or, I don't know...just everything!"

"Zoe thanks for not laughing. I don't want to be known as the weirdo who sees things."

"You are probably right to not talk about it. Some people would not get it. We'll keep this between us."

"For sure. This whole thing freaks out my mom. It's so not fair. I don't make imaginings happen. Moms are supposed to understand and support their kids. She's been acting extra whacky lately."

"Oh, that's too bad. What she doesn't understand scares her. Could it be something else is wrong?"

"Mom wanted us all to leave her alone. Dad and she have been arguing. He couldn't even wake me up to say goodbye when he dropped me off. Are they mad at me or mad at each other? I've even started thinking they might be divorcing."

"Oh don't even go there. Believe me, divorce is a major bummer for sure. My parents are divorced. Life isn't always fair. But heh, what was going on today at the farm?"

"Today was different. If I tell you, I'm afraid you will go back to thinking I'm crazy."

"I won't Lil, cross my heart and hope to die."

From their night nest, under the big night sky, Lillia told Zoe what she had heard and seen today.

Reaching up toward the stars and waving her hands in

circles, Zoe said, "It seems kind of magical like. Mysterious and magical things come to you. I wish the thing with the lady walking out of the photograph had happened to me."

"Good night, Zoe."

"Good night Lil."

Evening stars multiplied as the darkness deepened. Night sounds from the land, and the gentle lapping of the lake water lulled the girls to sleep as the stars and moon watched. In their innocent sleep, they dreamt

Many dreams have been dreamt on this land...hearts have held hopes close...fears were wrestled with...difficult losses were experienced.

Through it all, Mother Earth held her children in her arms and celebrated with them during their joys, soothed their fears, and comforted them during sorrow.

Lives lived on earth leave behind traces.

Like the astute detective gathers fingerprints, the intrepid hunter follows animal tracks, and the inquisitive scientist identifies DNA...there have always been those who can collect, analyze and interpret those fragments and particles of energy left behind. Lillia Pameroy was one of those in possession of such ability.

25

LILLIA

I woke to discover Zoe and Grauntie already up and about. Breakfast waited for me.

Zoe had convinced Grauntie Nora to take the house-boat to the flat-top rock. A bad feeling passed over me, but I shook it off. I would like to see a family cemetery too, just wished it wasn't with Emily. I couldn't wrap my mind around who, or what, she was. Why she showed up when and where she did?

I helped untie the boat from its moorings so Grauntie could back her out of the dock. She got her turned, pointed out toward the lake, and off we went.

I watched the flat-top rock get closer as we navigated along the shoreline. Approaching from the lake, I saw how enormous it was.

No strange vibes yet. No sounds of music. No campfire smells. No lady in a long dress.

Grauntie dropped anchor close to the shore. "Okay ladies, hop onboard the dingy and I'll take us to the shore."

There was a soft breeze, birds sang, fresh pine smells drifted by and hummingbirds darted about as we stepped onto the shore, pulling the dinghy up behind us so it couldn't drift away.

I saw Emily's bike leaning against the rock...an old rusty bike. Hey, wait a minute. Was it the same bike I saw zip past me outside of Tully's? Had that rider had been Emily?

I was struggling with telling the difference between an imagining and a real happening when Emily appeared, walking out from behind the rock. I watched her to see if she remembered anything about yesterday on the farm. No sign from her at all.

"Pleasure to meet you," she said, extending her hand to shake Grauntie's.

"Emily is it? It's so kind of you to agree to take us to a private family cemetery."

"My pleasure ma'am."

"Hey Emily...all right if we climb the rock first? It is way too tempting." Zoe pulled me along with her.

We started scrambling up the stone using rough hand-holds and small flat ledges to hoist ourselves up.

"Be careful," Grauntie called out.

From up top, I could see across the lake to White Cliff Landing. Up to the north of the town was a huge cliff...so pale in color, it was almost white. Now I saw where the name came from. Funny how, when you are so close to something, you see it differently. You miss the big picture.

This was the very spot the waving lady had been standing. This was the rock the Indians called a portal. I tried, but couldn't feel anything like Zoe thought I might.

Wish I could control my imaginings. Then they would be worth something in helping Miss Margaret. Everything was just too random now.

26

CEMETERY VISITOR

He had not been here for many years. His eyes scanned the road ahead for the turnoff. There it was. Signaling the turn and pulling off the main road, he steered his car onto the narrow gravel road.

He leaned further forward to peer over the steering wheel. The road was barely wide enough for one vehicle and it would not do to get his wheels off onto the softer edges and be stuck. No one would know he was here.

He had vague memories of visiting these graves as a child. Death is a part of life and he accepted it. Before he left this world, he yearned to see the sister he left behind when he fled so many years ago. He had fled the life his family lived. His mother grew up on a farm not far from here. His father, an unhappy and bitter man, worked long hours logging in the surrounding forests.

He had lost contact with his family after he left.

Sending many letters home, only to be disappointed when no response came back from them. His leaving had been hard, especially on his mother. He still remembered the night he left...storm raging, angry words spoken, tears streaming down his little sister's face.

He thought of the good life he had after he left for the big city on the ocean. He apprenticed with his father's brother, Uncle Theodore, and eventually took over the business. He loved a woman in the big city who had passed away many years ago. Wish I could have brought her here to rest he thought.

When the arch to the graveyard appeared ahead, he pulled over and shut off the engine. With his hands still gripping the steering wheel, he felt the familiar ache of loneliness inside. A constant reminder of what he had lost.

With a sigh, he reached across the seat for his wide-brimmed hat, placing it squarely on his head. He picked up the bouquet of flowers he had bought from Hattie. Getting out of his car, he walked toward the arch.

The woods here were a quiet cathedral, holding the prayers of the Indians, the soldiers, and the families. All people who had passed this way. Sad stories of broken lives, along with joyous stories of love and laughter shared.

He stopped to murmur a prayer before shuffling into the graveyard and entering under the arch, which had once held mounted wooden letters spelling his mother's family name.

He wandered among the headstones, silently paying his

respect. At a pair of narrow markers, he stopped and reached out to steady himself on one of the stones. He dropped to one knee, took off his hat, gently placed the bouquet on the grave, and said, "I miss you more than ever Mother and Father. May you rest in peace."

27

LILLIA

I enjoyed walking through the dense forest. It was cool, refreshing. Zoe and Emily were chatting as we walked along toward the cemetery.

I saw a shiny wavering in the trees off to my right. "Hey everyone, wait up a second. I see something over there."

"What to do you think you see?" Zoe asked.

"Not sure what it is, but it was like the sun hitting glass."

Bending and twisting, I peered between the forest's trees and shrubs for the source of the shining. There. I saw something again. A bounce of light from a window?

"Well I don't see a thing," Zoe said.

"Look closer. You have to catch sight of it between the tree trunks. It's past the big dead tree that looks like a skeleton."

"I understood there weren't any homes left on the LBL," Grauntie said as she joined us.

"Righto Lil. All gone. Cleared away. Big display at the visitor center. Remember, the house on the barge, just floating across the lake?" Zoe said.

"But come on, let's check it out."

Grauntie stared into the dense forest. I could tell she didn't see it. "Lillia, you must have been wrong. Let's keep going, the cemetery is right ahead. We can check it out on the way back."

Glancing back once more, I heard...

Later

"Yeah, come on let's head to the graves. That's why we're here, right Emily?" Zoe said.

Emily nodded thoughtfully. "Yep. You can check it out later. Later, when we come by this way again."

Long soft grass blades brushed my ankles as we left the dirt path. Insects scattered. Sunlight filtered down between the leaves on the trees. A breeze wound its way among the tree trunks as I walked toward the graveyard ahead.

In front of the graveyard was a beautiful old arch made of twigs and branches, hand woven to form the tall curving shape. From it hung a few sadly tilting wooden letters.

As we entered under the arch, I wondered whose family

lies buried in this cemetery. Did anyone still visit? It felt so sad and abandoned.

"Look at this place. Shady. Spooky. Dead quiet," Zoe said as she walked toward a grouping of small headstones. "These are little kids. So sad. Is this all one family buried here?"

"Yep, in a way. Probably related by marriage and such. Extended family, it's called," Grauntie said. "Let's be respectful. I know I am going to say a little prayer for those buried here. This is such a beautiful final resting place."

The cemetery was small. Roots of overgrown trees pushed up out of the earth, taking grave marker slabs with them. Grasses and small shrubs rambled where they chose. Moss blanketed the headstones. One upright marker leaned gently against another.

I found more headstones hidden among the roots of a big tree and lying underground hugging bramble, sunk into the earth.

The edges of the grave markers, once sharp and crisp, showed the effects of decades of weather. The names and dates, deeply etched in the stone slabs so many years ago, softened by time. *Beloved daughter, rest in peace, here lies a good man.* Some no longer legible, the letters felt by gently running my hand over the surface.

It was getting cooler. Now there was more shadowy darkness than light. No bird calls. No insect buzzes. A heavy stillness in the air.

I stood still...quiet...waiting. My eyes closed. Crush of sadness...old, dry, dead smells.

Then...

Lily scents...stirrings...low murmurings. Children's soft laughter. The air warmed. Slowly I opened my eyes.

The sunlight broke gently through the shadows. Insects stirred. Birds flitted overhead. Stones stood proudly upright. Trees behaved respectfully and kept their roots underground. Flowers bloomed in small plantings by the headstones.

A pretty, young woman watered flowers next to a marker. A tall boy raced by in front of me. Laughter followed as a young child ran after him.

The woman stood and called to the children. Her glance fell on me...me watching her. It was the lady from the photograph again...

These are my children
My family
They need you

Her mouth turned up softly and a sad smile formed before she began to fade away, along with the two children. Their laughter hung in the air a moment more before it too was gone.

Edges of markers slowly rippled back to weathered

stone. Flower petals shrank, drying to a thin crumbliness, and were caught by the breeze, shattering into pieces swirling and swimming past me, up to the heavens. The odor of bygone flowers lingered.

Zoe and Grauntie were still reading headstones a few rows over.

Emily was watching me. "Come over here Lillia. This grave has a fresh bouquet on it." She patted the marker and said, "It's good that there is still family around to come and visit Edna. Think she knows about it?"

"I think she does."

We all walked back under the wooden twig arch and started back down the path through the forest and toward the shore.

28

HOUSE IN THE WOODS

S *eventy-five years earlier...*

Tommy was leaving today.

Edna's hands clutched the front porch railing of the simple home. She looked down the stone edged path for signs of Pa returning from work. Lordy, but she hoped he would not argue with their son again. What went on within this house's walls last night had been awful.

Tommy was excited to be off and start his new life working with Uncle Theo in the big, faraway city. He decided to wait until Pa came home from his logging job to say one more goodbye. He hated leaving things so unsettled, so unhappy. There was Caroline, the doll he wanted to give his sister. He was saving that happy thing for last.

The air thickened with the approaching storm and treetops started twisting and bending in the strong winds.

Clouds blackened the sky and sunk the forest into a deep gloom. The house wished this would all blow over.

Edna felt the first raindrops and heard the distant rumbles of thunder as she watched Pa walking toward the house...an approaching thundercloud.

Now...

Lillia wanted to see what had caused the shining in the forest. Nora said, "The bugs are so bad now. I do not think it is a good idea. After all, no one else saw anything."

"But I want to look, just for a minute. You all can head back and I'll quick hurry and catch right up with you."

"I'll go with you," Emily said.

"Hey, so will I," Zoe added quickly. "I want to see it too."

"Well, if you all want to look for it, guess I can help too," Nora sighed.

Emily turned to Zoe and said, "Hope there are no snakes in here. Or poison ivy." Then she started making her way, pushing small branches aside and stepping through the underbrush.

What? Swatting at the bugs around her head, Zoe said, "Ouch, think I got a stone in my shoe. You guys go ahead." Snakes, she thought. Why hadn't I thought of that? Hate those creepy crawlies. No way I'm leaving this path.

Lillia, Emily, and Nora headed off deeper into the forest.

"Wait, don't go too far. Stop, I want to take a photo of you all in among the trees," Zoe shouted, but they kept walking. Dang, hope these shots take.

Nora came back in a few minutes. "Couldn't stand the bugs. Zoe, did you get the stone out?"

"Stone? Right. Yep, got it. Find the house?"

"I think Lillia saw the sunlight hitting something at a funny angle, though it does seem like there might have been a structure there once. But if there was a front yard, it's all grown over. Certainly no house left."

"Are they coming back now too?"

"Should be along shortly. Emily wanted to point something more out to Lillia. I hightailed it out of there."

Emily and Lillia were chatting and gesturing as they walked out of the forest. Best buds all of a sudden Zoe thought. So now, Emily's not so crazy? So odd?

"You guys find something?"

"Sort of. No real house left, but it did appear one had been there once," Emily said. "Trees planted in a row. Looked like a walkway. Right, Lillia?"

Lillia nodded.

"But no house? No glass? Hey, maybe it was moved away. Remember Lil? Like what we saw at the visitor's center." Zoe saw Lil wasn't listening. She looked so distracted. Same as at the cemetery. Something is going on yet again.

When the group arrived back at the shoreline, Nora

said, "Thanks so much for showing us the family burial ground Emily."

Zoe said, "It was kind of cool. There I go again. Cemeteries are serious stuff. Not cool. Interesting. Anywho, we're back to the shore now. So long!"

Lillia added, "Right. Thanks, Emily, I learned a lot. And I'll think about what you said."

Picking up her bike, Emily said, "Glad you decided to stop here today."

Lillia, Nora, and Zoe took the dinghy back out to the houseboat. Emily waved goodbye before pushing her bike into the dark forest and disappearing from view.

Her anchor was pulled up and the Lady of the Lake started back to White Cliff Landing.

"Feels like a storm is coming. Glad we'll be back in the home harbor all safe and sound. I imagine you girls will want to visit with Miss Margaret and chat about what you saw on LBL."

"I can't today. Promised Mom I'd help at the diner. Later I want to do some online research. How about tomorrow morning Lil?" Zoe asked.

"All right with you if I run over quick and tell her what we saw?" Lillia said. "She'll be waiting to hear."

Hey, aren't we in this together, Zoe thought. Why does she want to go so soon, and alone? Hiding stuff from me again. Something happened in the woods with Emily. Now she wants to get ahead of me and make it look like she's doing all the work.

"Guess I can ask Mom if I can get off, but don't see it happening. Been gone a couple of days now. First fishing, then the overnight. But you can go." Please please say we're in this together. Please don't go without me Zoe thought.

"Well, maybe...," Lillia hesitated.

"Lillia, would you like to go with me to take the clock to the TLC shop?" Nora quickly interjected

"Yeah, sure, okay. Suppose Miss Margaret can wait."

Well, Zoe thought, don't make it sound so tough. You aren't the one who has to go to work.

29

LILLIA

I started to unload the bikes as soon as we arrived back at the White Cliff Marina.

"Keep the bike. You've only got a couple of more days here, go ahead and use it," Zoe said, with a sharp toss of her backpack over her shoulder.

"If you're sure, that would be great," I said. Zoe seems upset. Thought we had an okay trip. What's bugging her now?

"Come on my little Lillia, let's find the key for this clock," Grauntie said as she came out carrying a blanket wrapped bundle.

Zoe pushed her bike alongside us as we walked up to Main Street. She was so quiet. "Zoe, didn't you say you met the clock man?"

"I see him around."

Now that was the shortest answer Zoe has ever given to a question.

Grauntie suggested we all get together at the diner tomorrow for lunch.

"Sounds okay," Zoe mumbled.

"We could work on the computer in the morning and see what we come up with. You're so good at all that stuff."

"Good idea. Hey, maybe Miss Margaret would like to come to the diner. You have a good Wi-Fi signal there, right? You could show her a few of the ancestry sites. She could bring her photos along, the ones she had in the old box. We've got to put our heads together. We'll work tomorrow morning if that's okay."

"Guess so," Zoe said.

"You never know what clue will point to the next thing. But right now Lillia, how about we let Zoe get to work and us to the clock shop?" Grauntie said.

"Glad I'm not going there with you."

"Why?" I asked.

"Just cause. Don't like the place."

Grauntie said, "Here you are Zoe. Thanks for coming with us on the trip."

"Thank you, I had a good time." Zoe walked in the diner's door without even saying a see you in the morning. What did I do to get her upset now? Like she said, I'm only here a couple of more days and I want to put the pieces together to solve our mystery.

We had stopped next to the old worn steps of TLC.

"I wonder what the TLC stands for? Tender Loving Clocks?"

"Not sure. Can you get the door for me? This clock is heavy."

A bell jingled above me as I pushed the door open. The creaking sounds echoed in the still and quiet place. A stir caused by the opening door moved the stale air apart, causing tiny dust specks to stir and swirl slowly in front of me. The old dry musty smell gagged me.

I had to wait for my eyes to adjust to the darkness before I could see a cone of light shining down on a scarred wooden surface further into the store.

"Hello?" Still holding the door, I leaned in.

"Go on in. I'm right behind you," Grauntie said.

Remembering Zoe's descriptions about the place, I decided to hold the door for Grauntie and let her be the one to go in first.

30

IN THE CLOCK SHOP

"Hello. Anyone here? Hellooo?" Nora saw Lillia staying by the door, and she could not blame her. This place was actually sort of, how did Zoe put it, creepy? Gloomy and dreary.

Lillia, peering in, said, "I see a light. Way back there."

"Guess I'll head that way. Come on along Lillia."

Nora saw clocks of all shapes and sizes populating the space. Interesting. Achoo. But dusty. This place sure could use a good airing out.

Hands appeared in the cone of light.

"Hello? We hoped you might be able to help us find a key to wind up this clock."

"Put it up here on the counter. I'll be right back." With those few words, the man disappeared into another room.

We looked wide-eyed at each other.

"Let's hurry up and get this done. This place gives me

the creeps. I feel like all the clocks are watching me," Lillia said.

"Well, it is called a clock's face."

"Ha-ha."

Carefully unwrapping her bundle, Nora said, "You know they don't make them like this anymore. Hope he can help us out."

One clock, then two, now all of them, started sounding...soft tick tocks, gentle cuckoos, and faint ding-dongs.

"What the...," Lillia blurted out.

As suddenly as the sounds started, they ended. No echo or reverberation, dead silence.

"Whew, now that was weird. Hope we're done here soon. I want to get out where I can breathe. This place is so choky and stuffy," Lillia said.

He returned carrying a small wooden box. There was a faint clattering sound as he set it on the counter. Pulling off the cover, he revealed a jumble of keys. He adjusted the work light lower over the box and reached for the clock.

He gave a soft gasp. The very air seemed sucked out of the room. His hands appeared to smooth as they hovered above the clock. With an aching slowness, he gently pulled it under the light.

Again the low, soothing, sighing sounds came. Comforting chimes and mellow gongs. The clock faces sparkled and gleamed, taking light and bouncing it around the dark shop.

Without raising his eyes, the man said, "Who does this clock belong to?"

"It's mine," Nora answered.

His sad, tired eyes looked up as he asked, "Do I know you?"

"I don't think so. I am Nora Pameroy. Here for the summer, staying on my friend Hattie's houseboat. Perhaps you know her. She runs the farmer..."

He interrupted in a frail voice. "Where did you get this clock?"

"On LBL in an antique store. Isn't it beautiful?"

He considered this information and with a slight tremor in his voice said, "This clock requires an unusual key. I will search for it later today. Can you please leave it with me? I promise to be careful."

"Let's get out of here. Let him keep it," Lillia said in a whisper from behind Nora's back.

"Sure you can keep it overnight. Should I stop back in the morning? Ah, I'm sorry didn't catch your name."

"Thomas."

"Better yet Thomas, how about I buy you lunch tomorrow for helping me to find the key?"

His eyes moistened and he replied, "That would be kind of you."

"Okay then, see you around noon at the diner," Nora grinned and gave a thumb up. "With a key, I hope."

He nodded and offered a small smile.

We headed out of the shop.

Thomas braced his hands on the counter to steady himself as his entire body sagged in toward the clock. He slowly reached under his shirt collar and pulled out a chain. At the end of it dangled a key. Pulling the chain off over his head, he grasped the key in his palm. With a slight moan and a bowed head, he closed both hands around the key and pulled it in toward his chest, cradling it against his heart.

31

LILLIA

I felt so clean out in the fresh air. I could breathe.

"Grauntie, why did you have to invite him to lunch?"

"I didn't have to, I wanted to. I thought it would be enjoyable."

"Oh." Now, what would be enjoyable about that? She always was so sweet like that. "Well, it was pretty nice of you. He seemed kind of lonely."

"And it was nice of him to accept. See how it works?"

To avoid a long discussion, I nodded.

"Hi, Peter."

"Hello, Nora. How was your trip to LBL Lillia?" Peter asked.

"Good. Saw a lot of stuff."

"The girls went to the Golden Pond visitor center and to the Home Place. Saw buffalo too. They learned how entire families and villages moved off LBL when the government made it a recreational area. The girls were looking for clues to help Miss Margaret find her family. She's from this area originally you know," Grauntie told him. "They are going to compare photos from there with ones she has and hope to find a connection."

"My grandmother left me a small box of old family pictures. I glanced at them once and packed them away. Would you gals like to see them? My kin used to live across the lake, running the village store. My family cemetery is still there."

Family cemetery? Maybe he knew more about the one we saw, I thought. "That would be great Mr. Pottle. In fact, one photo at the Home Place had the Pottle name on it."

"Really? That sure is interesting. I could bring my box of photos with me in the morning. Could we get together tomorrow?"

"Sounds good. We are going to meet Miss Margaret at the diner sometime late tomorrow morning. Could you come over too?" I asked.

"You bet. I'll hang my *Gone to Lunch* shingle in the door and join you there. Tomorrow then."

"See you later." Maybe this will work out and we will find a family for her after all.

Next door, Zoe was wiping down tables. I knocked on the window and waved. Guess she didn't see me because she turned and went back to the counter. I'll surprise you tomorrow with the news about Mr. Pottle. I will do my part.

Heading back to the marina, I saw LBL across the lake. All those imaginings must mean something. If I think more about them they might make some sense.

Grauntie Nora said, "I see you looking over at LBL. Its history goes way back. There are Civil War sites there..."

I told myself to focus on what I know for sure. Imaginings get me in trouble with Mom. She still thinks I don't know, I don't remember, but I do.

"...and so the Indians who survived, left there by the Trail of Tears. Now you see Lillia, there are stories everywhere and the clockmaker has a story too."

Oops, I wasn't paying attention. "Right Grauntie."

She smiled and gave me a little squeeze. "Glad you put up with your old grandaunt and her yakking. I know sometimes I put out too much information."

"It's all right. You have an inquisitive mind."

She let out a big laugh. "One way to put it. I want to share so much with you and Charlie. The world is such a wonderful place. Well, here we are. Going to heat us up some dinner. Want to help?"

"You bet."

Grauntie went to bed hours ago, but I was having a hard time falling asleep. I made a chocolate milk and sat at the little table. The windows were open and the night air felt good.

Wondered if Mom was still awake and staring at the

same moon? We hadn't talked this whole trip. I kept missing her calls and I didn't mind. I was afraid talking with her would spoil my time here.

Now, though, I spoke to her in my thoughts. Mom, sometimes I'm afraid of my imaginings too. I don't want to keep pretending. I'm tired. Wish you could help me. Isn't that what moms do?

Would she love me again if I showed her my imaginings could be used for good things?

Seeing the little doll inside Mom had come to me like things do...just happening in my head...like a thought that pops up. Yesterday the voice said when I see things I should believe them. The little four-year old me didn't know she was seeing a dead baby...she thought she was seeing a dolly. I did not know death when I saw it.

What had I seen in the woods today? Emily is a whole other thing to think about. She told me I had to go back to the place in the woods. It was important. She said I was special. It felt like she was helping me, guiding me. But, at the farm, I thought I saw her with the lady who wasn't real, who was only an imagining. The same lady who said her children needed me.

Should I go back to the woods?

Grabbing the sides of my head, I tried to shake my thoughts out, examine them, make sense of them.

Reasons not to go back to the place in the woods. One...I'd have to sneak out or lie to Grauntie. Two...I'd need to borrow a boat without asking permission.

Three...Mom would be so pissed I'm even thinking about doing this. Four...if I got into an imagining alone in the woods I might not get out. Five...no one would know where to look for me. Reasons to go there. One...

Ugh, I'm tired and just want to fall asleep. Tomorrow is another day.

I dreamt about home. I was there alone and I couldn't find anyone else. I was locked in and windows and doors would not open. I was frantic.

Coming across the back lawn, though the trees, I saw Tucker with Charlie and a little girl riding on her back. His fingers gripped the fur around Tucker's neck. Walking alongside them was Grandpa. His head swiveled and he looked at me with spooky, pale green eyes. They all waved at me as they walked by and out to the road.

I pounded on the windows. Don't go! I'm here. Wait!

They kept walking toward the street. They joined a group of marching people. I saw Hattie, Peter Pottle, and Elvira. Then Julia and Zoe. Everyone was leaving.

Again I tried to shout no, don't go. Home is here. I'm home. My dream voice came out just above a whisper and they all kept marching away.

32

STORM COMING

Dark storm clouds loomed on the horizon. Distant thunder rumbled ominously through the faraway hills. Winds pushed a path ahead of the storm, bending treetops and lifting the fleeing birds.

Peter erased yesterday's Nutty Banana Twirl and added Jazzy Rainbow Sherbet to his sign. Looking toward the approaching storm, he decided to pull the sign board inside. Heading back out, he struggled to anchor the flapping awning more securely.

Thomas had had another restless night. His dreams were so vivid. He dreamt he had lost the clock key and desperately hunted for it, one of those futile, endless, searching dreams.

He dressed before finishing his morning coffee, all the while trying to think of what to say to Nora. How could he tell her the very key she needs is right against his heart? He had made the decision to try to buy the clock from her. Afterward, he would go over to the shop where she bought it and try to get more information on it.

Julia felt the change of pressure in the air brought on by the approaching storm. She was glad Zoe was staying inside today.

The harbormaster had seen the girl leave on the little boat, surprised she was allowed out on the lake with the storm threatening. Could it be she didn't want anyone to know she was going and had not asked for permission? Had the spirits called to her?

Ring, ring, ring.

Nora picked pulled her cell phone out of her jean pocket. "Hello."

"Good morning Nora, this is Margaret."

"Oh, good morning. Sure looks a big storm blowing in doesn't it?"

"Yes, it does. I will be heading down soon to meet with the girls at the diner. Hope the rain holds off for my walk. I wanted to chat a minute if that's okay."

"Sure."

"Nora, the reason I called concerns Lillia. Please forgive me if I'm putting my two cents worth in where it doesn't belong, but she's such a sweet girl."

"What is it?"

"I have a strong sense Lillia has perceptions of the world that go much deeper than ours."

Nora's ears perked up. She put her coffee cup down. "Go on."

Margaret continued. "From the first time I met her on my front porch, I had the sense that our paths were meant to cross. She possesses something unique and our dance on the houseboat confirmed it."

"It did?"

"The music was coming from another time," Margaret said. "Through her, I could again hear the tunes my father's family played. Do you find that impossible to believe?"

Nora took a deep, calming breath and said, "No Margaret, I don't."

"Oh good. My instincts told me to reach out to Lillia, but I am not sure why. Do you know why Nora?"

"I think I might. Let me give you a little history. From the moment Lillia spoke, I knew she was different. She would be playing, turn to glance across the room, and say, 'No David, you can't do that,' then calmly go back to her play. She would ask her mommy to please tell the little girl upstairs I would like to play with her kitty when there was no one else living in their house."

"But don't most little children play pretend and have imaginary friends?"

"This was always felt different. My brother, God rest his soul, had special talents too. He could never explain them to me. He would quote Maya Angelou, 'Talent is like electricity. We do not understand electricity. We use it.'" Nora said.

"So I was right to feel Lillia is different?"

"Yes. I am not sure exactly how her gifts work. However, I think one way is that she makes connections with life energies of people who are gone. I believe there are phenomena all around. Things humans cannot understand, or comprehend. That doesn't mean they aren't real. Like a woman's intuition. Or the feeling when the hairs stand up on the back of your neck."

Margaret said, "And I believe there are certain places on our earth able to hold memories longer. That is partly why I came back here. I wanted to be nearer the place that held my family's history. I'm hoping it will help me find them."

"I feel that places have some sort of interaction with people like Lillia."

"Cemeteries?" Margaret asked. "Or old houses people think are haunted?"

"Yes, those types of places, but they don't have to be scary or spooky. LBL has such an emotionally powerful history so I think it might be one of those places."

"Oh, I'm so relieved you know about this too. Particularly after my dream about her last night,"

"What dream?"

"I was much younger, alone and scared. I saw Lillia with my old doll. It was as if she was trying to get to me but stayed just out of reach. It was so real that when I woke in the middle of the night, I got my doll and slept holding her...like I must have done as a young girl."

"That is such a sweet story. Guess we all had something to hug and sleep with when we were young."

"I'm a strong believer in responding to feelings, intuitions, and dreams. I'm supposed to meet Zoe and Lillia later at the diner. I'll bring Caroline with me."

"Caroline?"

"My doll."

"Oh! Cute. I'm meeting someone for lunch there too. So I'll see you and Caroline soon."

"Bye Nora."

33

LILLIA

I decided to go back. I knew Grauntie wouldn't let me go by myself and I didn't want Zoe going with me in case things went badly. So I told no one and went alone.

I felt bad taking Julia's boat. Sometimes it was better to ask forgiveness than permission.

Starting across the lake, I heard the thunder as it rolled over the hills. I hoped the wind wouldn't make the lake too rough for me to get back later.

I landed the boat on the shore near the flat-top rock and headed into the woods.

The leaves of the shrouding trees caught the first rain-drops. Around me, the insect sounds grew louder.

The white skeleton tree glowed against the dark forest. The house should be off to my right.

Ahead trees formed two rows. Stepping cautiously, I entered the path between them.

Close on each side of me, among the wild forest grasses, I saw stacks of fieldstone. Path walls? The grasses bend over the stones, yielding as the rain hit them.

The storm had arrived, treetops swaying and twisting above me.

My clothes pushed wet against me as I paused. Was this a bad idea? What was I looking for?

I told myself to wait. Don't push. Be patient. Let it come to you.

Then, between the relentless beats of the falling raindrops, moaning cries of the whipping wind, and harsh rumbles of the distant thunder...another sound.

Something else... almost human.

I held my breath, rooted to the spot.

34

MISSING

"Hey, Nora. How are you today?" Julia asked.

"Fine. How about you?"

"Okay, but I could use a coffee break, want to join me."

Nora replied, "Sure. How are the girls doing on their Margaret project?"

Julia poured two cups of coffee at the counter and set one down in front of Nora.

"Umm, not sure. Let me run up and see if Zoe has found anything on her computer," Julia said. "I don't think Lillia is here yet," she added from halfway up the stairs.

Not here yet? Nora nervously peered out the front window.

Whump! A bird hit hard against the glass, startling her.

The rain started.

Zoe came down the staircase talking with her mom. As they entered the diner, Nora heard Zoe saying, "...there was a horrible storm and people were killed. Can you believe it? In a stupid storm? So any-who, there was this Lewis family. The mom and dad were found dead and their poor little daughter was found wandering in the forest."

Julia said, "Oh my, you've learned a lot."

"I'm thinking the little girl might be Miss Margaret. Fingers crossed. The article said the couple had an older son, but his body was never found. He disappeared. Wouldn't it be great if he was still alive?"

"Zoe honey, take a breath. Bet you can't wait to tell her about it."

Before Zoe could answer Nora said, "Zoe, have you seen Lillia? She said she was spending the day with you."

"No. Haven't seen her. Got lots of stuff to show her."

Seeing the concern on Nora's face, Julia said, "Everyone must have gotten their wires crossed. She's probably back at the houseboat waiting for you."

Zoe thought, darn her anyway. I bet Lil went behind my back to talk to Miss Margaret.

Nora knew something was not making sense. "You might be right. Think I'll run back and see if she's there."

Stepping out onto the sidewalk under the darkening sky, Nora heard distant rumblings. Lightning illuminated the insides of the approaching thunderheads.

She bumped into Peter hurrying over to the diner. He juggled a box with one hand and his umbrella with the other.

"I saw you heading into the diner. I'm so excited.

Found tons of good photos. My Granny wrote names on the back of them."

"Oh, wonderful. The girls will be so pleased. Why don't you get in out of this rain? Zoe is inside. I have to run to the boat for something."

She raced through the wind and rain. Surely, Lillia was from back wherever she had gone and this was all a misunderstanding.

"Excuse me, ma'am."

Nora jerked her hand off the houseboat railing, shifting her eyes to find the voice's source.

"Didn't mean to startle you," a man said, stepping out of the gray wet gloom. "The young girl who lives here with you...?"

Where had she seen this stranger before? "Yes go on. What is it? Have you seen her?"

"Yes, I did and thought I should let you know."

"Please, step in out of the rain. I am sorry, but I can't place you. Do we know each other?" Nora asked.

"I'm the fella who takes care of things here in the harbor area. Name is Degataga. But people call me Dega."

"I'm Nora. Now where is it you saw my grandniece?"

"Saw her leaving the harbor on the diner lady's fishing boat. Looked to be headed across the lake."

35

LILLIA

I felt the edge of the stonewall. Must touch something I know is real.

What was forming in front of me faded in and out of focus with a low moaning.

Voices now, somewhere outside of me but inside of my imagining.

At my feet, ghostly porch steps taking shape. I could feel them pushing against me, forcing me to decide. Step back and go away or step up and move inward through the thin veil.

I lifted one foot to test the first step. It looked weak and fragile. It held me. Two more steps and I stood on a wooden surface. Porch?

Something waited for me.

A front door, now completely formed, slowly swung open.

A house should not be here, but it was.

I stepped into my imagining.

I was inside a large open room with a stone fireplace to my left. I could smell damp ashes as the rain tumbled down the open chimney.

Across the room, a door opened to a rear porch. On it stood a young man watching the storm rage.

To my right, a stairway was forming. The hint of someone coming down the staircase. Her form filled in. A child, plain dress, hair held with a ribbon. I heard her crying, "Momma, momma?"

Threatening thunder sounds shook the walls around us.

Suddenly a woman appeared and scooped her up. Cradling and comforting her with mothering hushes. The woman quickly put the girl on steps again and tried to shoo her back upstairs.

With fearful eyes, the child looked out the back door and shook her head no.

The woman brushed past me, fretful hands pushing strands of hair back from her face. She was the woman in the photo...the lady from the cemetery...

...help...

The winds swirled through the house...in out open windows open doors...heavy with the rain's wild wetness.

Thunder clapped and cracked...powerful vibrations.

Chimney flue funneled the blue energy of lightning to the hearth...cold glows below the mantel clock.

The storm outside swelled.

Window curtains yanked by the strong snapping, angry twisting of the frenzied wind.

The rain, with unearthly power, pounded against the frail shingles, trying to get in.

Black silhouette...another man outside...fists clenched, angry shouts.

"No Tom. I will not allow it. You will not leave. This is nonsense. Your family needs you here. I will not have it."

"You can't stop me, Father. I must do this. I am sorry you feel this way, but I am leaving. I will have a trade. I will make you proud."

With an earsplitting blast, lightning struck. I heard the sharp cry of the splintering, breaking limbs as they wrenched away from the tree.

36

WHAT ZOE KNEW

The harbormaster saw the woman's breath quicken, eyes widen and hands begin to tremble.

"What are you saying? My Lillia is out there in a boat all by herself on an awful day like this?" Nora said, her voice rising in volume.

Faltering, he answered, "At first, when I saw her leaving, I believed you had given permission."

"How could it be okay?"

He cast his eyes down. "Ma'am, people nowadays don't like others interfering in their business."

Nora could not believe what she was hearing.

"Then the storm moved in fast and I figured I'd best tell you about what I saw."

Her breath caught. "Of course. I'm sorry for yelling at you. Thank you for coming to me. I need to figure out what to do now."

Lightning slashed across the dark sky and a blast of thunder rocked the heavy air.

"How long ago did you see her leave?"

"More than an hour ago. She probably didn't see the storm moving in."

At that moment, the door spun open and a rain drenched Zoe pushed into the houseboat.

"Zoe, what are you doing here?"

Zoe bent over gasping for breath. "I know where Lil might be and I ran to tell you."

"Okay, catch your breath. Dega here was telling me he saw her leaving with your mother's fishing boat."

"Oh no. I was afraid of that. Remember the house we couldn't see?"

"What house?"

"In the woods by the cemetery. The Emily girl. She pushed her to go to the house. Oh please. You've got to find her."

"Emily? The girl we met? What about her?" Nora asked.

"She's not on the picture. She's not there," Zoe said.

"What picture?"

"I took a photo with my cell phone. Of you all. In the woods. I downloaded the photos to my computer. Emily is gone. She is not in it. She is not real. Lil went back. Back to find the house."

"Why in heaven's name would she do that? Are you sure Zoe? Why didn't you say something sooner?"

"I'm a bad friend. I told her she needed to tell the truth.

That she had to help. But it's Emily. She's tricky...she did it to Lil. Please find her...," Zoe sobbed. "I'm so sorry."

I saw the angry old man turn and with a sharp wave of his hand at his son, he said, "Good riddance." He charged into the house. "If he wants to go Edna, so be it. I'm done with him."

He stomped past her and out to the front porch, his cold dark eyes searching to see what damage the storm had done.

The young man entered the room and the woman reached to hug him. She started sobbing as he gently held her.

"Mother, I'm sorry it has come to this. You must understand I need to leave this place."

"Son, write me as soon as you get to your Uncle Theodore's. I will not rest until I know you are safe with him. I pray you will return home one day, until then, may God hold you safely in his hands."

"I will write Mother. I will miss you and Sissy very much...and I will even miss Pa."

The young man left to go upstairs. The little girl, still sitting on the third step, reached for him.

Another strike flashed, the entire forest around the house lit up as thunder boomed.

He picked the girl up, trying to make her laugh as he carried her up the stairs. With tears still clinging to her cheeks, she gave him a small grin and wiggled in his hold. He put her down on the top landing.

"Sissy, I have something for you, to keep you company until I can come back. Wait right here."

He returned with a traveling bag and a doll. Holding the doll with one hand, he made it dance in front of the little girl. She smiled and reached for it.

With one finger, he tapped his cheek and she stood on tiptoes to kiss him as he gave her the doll.

"I named her Caroline. It means song of happiness. Sissy, you are my happiness and I will sing your name on all my travels. So when you hold Caroline close and listen carefully, you will hear me singing."

The young man set his valise on the landing to straighten his suspenders. He took a wide brimmed hat from the coat rack and pulled it over his head.

He looked at the clock on the mantle. He hurried to it and removed the key, slipping it quickly into his pocket.

He left, walking out the back door, off the porch steps, and into the furious storm.

I could hear the couple arguing on the front porch.

"Please, he's our son. We shouldn't part this way."

"Leave me alone woman. I have more important things to worry about."

I felt the strength of wasted, unnecessary anger. I wanted to tell him no, go to your son, you are a family.

38

FINDING LILLIA

Dega slowly shook his head side to side and whispered, "Haunted."

Nora spun sharply to face him. "What? What did you say?"

"I said haunted. The area around the flat-top rock is haunted. Some say they have seen a spirit there. People hear old time music coming from the rock. It was a sacred site to the Indians, a portal to the spirit world."

"Lillia saw that lady and heard the music there too," Zoe exclaimed.

"If Lillia's gone there we must get to her! She might be in danger. She's not ready to handle things, all alone in such a place," Nora cried.

"But how? It would be crazy take a boat in this storm," Zoe said.

"I know the way by road, over the north bridge," Dega

said. "I'll take my pickup truck and head out. Can someone come with me? She will be afraid. She doesn't know me."

"I'll go with you," Nora said. "Zoe you run back and let your mother know what is going on. Hurry now."

Nora and Dega dashed through the rain to his truck.

Zoe, hands shielding her eyes, ran back to the diner.

"Mom, Mom, Lil's missing. I think she's gone to find the abandoned house. But it's not there. And the place is haunted. She's all alone and it's all Emily's fault," Zoe blurted out as soon as she saw her mother. "I knew there was something wrong with her."

"Zoe, calm down. What's this about?" Julia asked, grabbing Zoe by the shoulders.

With tears streaming down, Zoe said, "I should have known. She wasn't telling me stuff. Emily is not real. What is she? Lil went alone in this awful storm. Her grauntie and some guy are headed over to find her."

Julia said. "She'll be fine. It's a storm. They'll find her."

"It's not the storm I'm worried about."

A blast of wind blew napkins about as Hattie and Delcie entered the diner, struggling to close the door behind them.

"Lordy but it's a big one blowing in," Delcie said. "Glad you got the stand buttoned up good."

Hattie, shaking herself like a wet dog, laughed. "Hope it is. Now let's get that cup of coffee you promised me and watch the storm pass through.

"Julia, what's wrong with the child?" Hattie asked when she saw how upset Zoe was.

"Lillia's gone missing. We think she took a small boat across to LBL," Julia answered.

"This is an awful day to be on the lake. My goodness, what was she thinking?" Delcie said.

"It's a long story, I'm not exactly sure, but Nora's gone over there to try to find her." Turning back to Zoe, Julia said, "Honey, Mr. Pottle and Miss Margaret are there in the corner booth going over the photos. Why don't you see what they've discovered?"

A thundering boom and lightning strike spilt open the sky. The rain pummeled the sidewalk.

Inside the diner, Thomas sat quietly in the corner, listening to the goings on.

Outside a big black car entered White Cliff Landing, driving slowly through the downpour.

LILLIA

39

LILLIA

I tried to hold my place as the walls of the house start to waver and moan...

...help them...

Then suddenly the house calmed. It hung suspended in its journey between worlds.

The little girl slowly started down the steps, the doll tucked in by her side. Her dress swirled around her tiny body.

She extended her small, delicate hand out to me and I tried to touch it. I felt like I was moving but could not reach her.

The howling wind pushed through the thin walls now. The house was leaving and the rain fell in.

She let out a surprised cry as a blast of wind ripped the ribbon from her hair.

40

STRANGE WOODS

The truck's headlight beams pushed through the curtain of rain, searching for the road to the flat-top rock.

"There it is," Dega said, as he slowed the truck and turned down the old gravel road. The truck lurched, tilting near the edge of the roadbed. "Sorry. Hang on Nora. This road doesn't go all the way, but it'll get us close,"

Nora grabbed the dashboard to brace herself as he cranked the steering wheel sharply.

She said a quick prayer that Lillia would be found soon. Hard telling how scared she was...all alone in this frightful weather. More than the storm, though, Nora feared what Lillia would encounter in this place. Would she be able to handle what was waiting for her in these strange woods?

41

LILLIA

I saw her ribbon twisting and spinning, dancing around me while thunderclaps spilt the air between us, urgent and angry.

Her image grew fainter.

I saw the wind whipped trees through the thinning skin of the house. The misty, softening, floating walls were disappearing.

She was drifting away now. Back up the vanishing staircase.

Her small hand still reached out to me.

An impossibly loud crash, followed by screams, enveloped me.

The trees swayed and churned, moved by the powerful winds.

Suddenly it all stopped. The imagining was over and I was left standing alone in the woods.

No wait...come back...let me help you.

I heard, "Lillia, it's Grauntie. I'm by the skeleton tree. Are you here?"

In a daze, I turned to the sound of her voice.

"Lillia! Lillia!"

42

DINER GATHERING

The storm hung suspended over the village. Rain fell in blowing sheets across Main Street. Boats in the harbor tugged at their lines, struggling in the wind-whipped waters.

The awning over Pottle's front door had loosened again. It beat with harsh snaps as the wind pushed against it.

Inside the Main Street Diner Zoe listened to the conversations buzzing around her...no storm like this in years...hope the river don't rise too much...this'll knock out the crops...sure you can warm up my coffee...cozy in here. All background noise...where is she? What kind of person am I?

With a rush of wind and rain, the front door snapped open. The man had to push hard to close it. He brushed rain from his shoulders and pulled back the hood of a young boy with him. Looking around the diner, they decided to take a table at the back. The boy jumped into one seat as the man took off his coat and sat in the other.

An extra loud thunderclap startled everyone.

Against the back wall, Thomas watched as he sipped his coffee.

Zoe decided she might as well go over and see the photos Mr. Pottle had brought.

Miss Margaret offered a hug. "Zoe, you seemed so worried. I heard you telling your mom about Lillia. I am sure her Grauntie Nora will find her safe and sound. Meanwhile, look here. Peter has all of these family photos from his grandmother. We were getting started looking at them"

Peter showed her the one he was holding.

Zoe took out her cell phone and flicked her fingers across the screen until she came to the photo of the framed picture at the farmhouse. The one Lillia had been staring at before she got all hinky. "I took a photo of a photo at the farmhouse. Looks like it was taken at the same time as yours."

"Why it surely does," Miss Margaret said. "Now let me see, can you zoom in Zoe? Hmmm, looks like it says the Hellerman and Pottle family reunion. Why I'll be darn."

Peter said, "Lillia said something to me about that photo." He gave a hoot as he pointed excitedly at the back of the photo he was holding. "This has writing on the back. Maggie is a nickname for Margaret, right? My Granny wrote 'My cousin Edna Hellerman Lewis, Tommy, and

Maggie'. Could we be looking at a photo of you Miss Margaret?"

"Oh, my. Could it be me?" A soft moisture gathered in the corner of her eyes. "And this might be my mother? And my brother?"

43

LILLIA

I heard the call again.

"Lillia, are you here honey? It's Grauntie."

No more house, or family, or clock, or girl. At my feet lay her hair ribbon, wet and twisted. I quickly picked it up and tucked it in my jean pocket before calling out, "Over here."

"Where? I can't see you," she shouted back over the howling wind.

I said in a low whisper, "Goodbye little girl. Now I know your story."

I left, running through the forest and into Grauntie's arms. Next to her was the man from the marina.

She covered me with her jacket and hurried me to a pickup truck parked nearby.

"Whatever were you up to all alone out here? You gave me an awful scare."

The truck bounced and slid its way along the narrow road out of the woods.

"I am so glad we found you. This wasn't the type of adventure I pictured us having on this visit," Grauntie said, drying me off with a big soft towel.

"Me either. I'm sorry I frightened you. But I had to come back here."

"Why Lillia? In a storm? Not telling anyone?"

"Well, it's sort of a long story. I needed to sort some things out for myself."

"And I want to hear all about it sweetie, but right now what I want to tell you is you were wrong to go off on a boat all by yourself, without letting anyone know."

"Sorry."

"If it hadn't have been for Dega seeing you leave, and Zoe knowing where you might have gone, it could have been a long time before we found you."

How did Zoe know where I was going I wondered?

"Thank you, sir."

We walked into an unbelievable, but the very real scene. The diner was full of people. Everyone was chattering, smiling and laughing. Zoe was the first to see us and she screeched with happiness as she rushed over to hug me.

"Lil, Lil, Lil! You're safe. I'm so glad. I'm so mad. How could you go by yourself and not tell me? It wasn't right you know." Zoe told me as she hugged me again. "But I'm not really mad. Relieved to see you. Can you believe it?

Peter Pottle and Miss Margaret are cousins. Her nickname was Maggie. And her parents died in a storm."

The news fit with what I had seen. A woman and man died today...that day...the day I had just left. The brother never even knew...he never turned back toward his home as he walked away.

"I need to tell you what happened to me in the woods. I found the house and I had an imagining. I think...."

"Excuse me, girls. Lillia, there is someone here to see you. Right this way," Grauntie said as she gently guided me toward the back of the diner.

Next thing I knew, I was lifted off my feet and held in my father's arms. Charlie started dancing and cheering beneath me.

"Daddy! You're here. Oh, I'm so happy to see you. And you too Charlie." I gave Daddy the biggest squeeze I could.

"Lilly, Lilly...are you okay? I missed you and I dreamt you were all alone in a boat on a stormy lake," Charlie said to me.

"Yes Charlie," I answered, "I am okay."

"Looks like you are part of quite a busy afternoon," Dad said.

I hugged him tighter. I closed my eyes as tears of relief threatened to spill from them. Wiggling out of his arms I said, "Daddy, I'll be right back. I have to talk to a lady over there."

"Lillia, I am so happy to see you are safe." Miss Margaret said as she squeezed my hand. "Here, I'll scoot over. Sit with us a minute. Peter, can I move this bag to your side?"

Peter reached for it as he said, "Me too. We were all so worried about you."

"Have you heard? Peter and I are cousins. We figured out his grandmother was a Hellerman and so was my mother. Zoe is going to start putting together a family tree."

"Oh, that is wonderful news. You found family," I said.

"Right," Peter added. "Now Margaret can meet more of her extended family too. I'm so pleased."

"My Dad and brother are here, so I might be leaving today instead of tomorrow. Miss Margaret, I know this sounds weird, but is the doll you showed Zoe and me named Caroline?"

She sat up straight and wide-eyed before she said, "Why yes that is her name. But how did you know?" Then she turned and motioned for Peter to hand her the bag back. She reached in and pulled out Caroline.

CAROLINE

44

CAROLINE

Thomas took another sip of his coffee and decided he would leave in a minute. With all the goings on, it would be best he talked to Nora about the clock on another day.

Outside the darkest part of the storm had passed. Rain was still falling lightly. Already the sun peeked out. A rainbow formed over the cloud-filled sky across the lake.

Zoe took Caroline from Peter. "She's beautiful. Don't her eyes seem real? Oh and the eyelids work. Blink, blink."

Thomas stood, settling his wide-brimmed hat on his head, and turned to leave. He caught sight of the doll.

The group's attention stayed focused on the doll Zoe was playing with. They did not notice the old man staring at it. With unsteady, halting steps, Thomas started walking toward the booth.

Softly he murmured, "Sissy." Then with more strength and in a singsong voice, "Little Sissy of mine."

Margaret looked up, confused. Who was singing those words? An old stooped man was walking across the room toward her.

Everything in the diner faded to a blur. Was he calling her Sissy? With weak knees, she rose from her seat. Conversation in the diner stopped. All eyes were on her and the man who was but a few steps away now.

"It's me," he said. "Your big brother Tommy."

The veil of time parted and she remembered. Margaret clutched her hand to her chest. Peter leaped up to steady her. She spoke softly, "Tommy?"

"Sissy, I'm home."

I smiled. This was so right.

It was Thomas Lewis, her brother, right here this whole time. Less than an hour ago in our time, but many years in imagining time, I saw him give Caroline to his sister. Now I saw them all together again.

With a quick glance to the heavens, I thought that now, lady on the rock, you can be at peace. No longer unsettled and wandering the land. Your family is together again, right here in the Main Street Diner in White Cliff Landing, Kentucky.

Miss Margaret had called our meeting and the music thing serendipity. Luck? Timing? Fate? I still do not know how this all came together, but it did and that is what is important.

Part of it was because Grauntie was so sweet to get a

clock for Hattie, one that happened to be missing a key. That took us to the clockmaker. She invited him to lunch so he was at the diner and saw Caroline.

Funny how things go.

THE RAINBOW

On the horizon, a rainbow quietly washed the sky with color. The storm had passed. The sun shone again in White Cliff Landing.

Zoe had everyone laughing as she described the look on Lil's face when she first saw Caroline. "You should have seen yourself. Your eyes were huge and kept blinking like the doll's eyes. It was so funny. I'm just a rockin' her back and forth. Open...close. Blink blink. Poor Caroline is thinking enough already. Hey you, big brother, step up, help me out here!"

"And up he walked. Now remember Zoe, you were the one who thought dolls were creepy," Lillia replied with a grin.

"And that they hold spirits. This one sure did. Waited decades to see Tommy again. She probably thought you'd never show up."

Smiling at his little sister, Tommy said, "I still can't believe I'm sitting next to Sissy."

"It surely is a wonderful blessed thing." Miss Margaret said. "Thank you to Zoe and Lillia, my two wonderful wizards who helped me reunite with my cousin Peter and my dear brother Tommy."

"I am so happy we are all here together to share your joy," Nora said. She felt certain Lillia and her specialness were the key to all of this.

Thomas patted Margaret gently on the arm and excused himself, "I have something I need to get. There is one last thing to do. I'll be right back."

47

LILLIA

I watched everyone together here in the diner. We all had a share in bringing Thomas the clockmaker and our Miss Margaret back together. Tommy and Sissy.

Dad and Charlie looked so good sitting with Grauntie. I need to appreciate family more...no one, no family, is perfect. I cannot wait to see Sam and Tucker again, and to sleep up under the eaves in my own bed.

As for Mom, I knew she loved me, and I knew she feared me. Guess I'd have to live with that.

Thomas returned carrying the clock. He set it down on the table in front of me. From around his neck, he took off a chain that held a key and handed it to me. "Would you do the honors Lillia?"

He still had the key! I paused for but a second, to take in the smiling faces and the feelings of friendship and family in this room, before I took it from him, inserted it and started winding.

48

CALM AFTER THE STORM

In the Main Street Diner, Julia and Zoe wiped down tables and cleaned up after the busy afternoon. They simply could not believe what a wonderful day it had been. Zoe and Lillia exchanged phone numbers and emails addresses with promises to keep in touch.

The Smithton brothers left to retrieve Julia's boat from the LBL shore where Lillia left it. Julia promised them an extra special meatloaf dinner when they got back.

Peter unfurled his awning, ducking and laughing as the rain water trapped in it splashed down to the sidewalk.

The water just missed Sissy and Tommy who sat on Peter's bench enjoying their Rainbow Sherbet cones. They had so much catching up to do.

Margaret told Thomas she loved that he had named his shop after their uncle. She would help him in the Theodore Lewis Clock shop by washing windows and shining up the clocks. He promised to throw the windows and doors wide open to bring in the fresh air and sunshine.

Peter talked about them all going for a visit to LBL. They could check out the photo at the Home Place and of course, go to see the family cemetery.

After a while, they all sat quietly, watching the rainbow and letting the wonders of the day sink in.

Adam drove down to the marina to pack up Lillia's things for the drive back home to Kansas. Nora decided to enjoy the rain-freshened evening air and walk back to the marina with Charlie and Lillia.

49

LILLIA

I saw the harbormaster resting on his bench. He rose as we approached. "Evening ma'am, Lillia."

"Hello, Dega. This is Charlie, my grandnephew. Thank you again for everything," Grauntie said.

"You are welcome."

Charlie blurted out, "Are you an Indian?"

A groan escaped from my lips. "Charlie! It's Native American."

"Oops sorry."

"Either name is fine Charlie."

"Does your name mean wolf or something?" Charlie asked.

"Charlie, don't be rude," Grauntie said.

"It is fine. My name is Degataga. It means to stand firm. In the Cherokee language, the word for wolf is waya."

"Waya...cool. I'm going to tell my friends I met a real Indian."

"I too will remember I met you, your sister and your grandaunt. And that it was a good thing."

I smiled. "Thank you. I don't know what would have happened if you hadn't driven Grauntie over to find me."

"Tsi lu gi. You are welcome," Dega replied as he handed me a piece of paper. "And here, Ernest Smithton found this old menu in the boat. Thought it might be yours or Julia's."

"That was nice of him, but it's not mine," I said, handing the menu to Grauntie. "

"Well isn't this the strangest thing?" she said.

"What is it?"

"The way this reads, it's from Mimi's Cafe. Many years ago, in Bon Secour, there was a cafe with this name."

"Hmm, I wonder how it ended up in Julia's boat."

"It does remind me I've been planning to volunteer as a docent at a historical home there in a few months. Perhaps you and Charlie can join me. It's on the Alabama gulf coast."

Then Dega handed me an envelope. "A girl stopped by and asked me to give this to you. She said to tell you safe travels."

"A girl? What did she look like?" I asked.

"She had short hair and beautiful pale green eyes."

Grauntie said, "Must have been Emily. I am sorry we missed her. Zoe was going on about her not being real or some such thing. Now wasn't that silly?"

I tucked the envelope in my pocket and my hand twirled around the wet ribbon. "Yes, it was Grauntie, very silly."

ALSO BY BRENDA FELBER

ABOUT THE AUTHOR

ABOUT THE AUTHOR

Please visit my website for photographs and additional information on Land Between the Lakes in Kentucky, Pameroy Mystery Series, and me!

I look forward to hearing from readers of *Unsettled Things*! Feel free to drop me a note with your thoughts or questions. If you travel to Land Between the Lakes and visit some of the sites, take a photo of yourself and send it to me. I always enjoy hearing from readers!

Happy reading...

Brenda Felber

www.pameroymystery.com
brenda@brendafelber.com

![f]

Made in the USA
Middletown, DE
17 July 2018